Fanie Viljoen is a well-known
Afrikaans South African
author, living in Bloemfontein.
A full-time writer, illustrator
and artist, Fanie has written
numerous short stories, radio
plays and books for children
and teenagers. Several of these
books have won awards for
children's and youth literature
in South Africa.

IN THE SAME SERIES

Scarred Lions

FANIE VILJOEN

Ransom

Scarred Lions
FANIE VILJOEN

Series Editor: Peter Lancett

Published by Ransom Publishing Ltd.
Radley House, 8 St. Cross Road, Winchester, Hampshire, SO23 9HX, UK
www.ransom.co.uk

ISBN 978 184167 7521

First published in 2011
Copyright © 2011 Fanie Viljoen.
Front cover photograph © manfredxy.

This book could not have been
written without the kind help of
the following people:

Marita, Carel and Annemarie
van Aswegen,

Hanlie and Riana Haasbroek,

but especially Hannes
Haasbroek, whose superior
knowledge of the South African
animal and plant life helped
form the backdrop to this.

Main characters

Buyisiwe (meaning returned)
Teenage boy, narrator

Themba (meaning trust, hope, faith)
Father, game ranger

Lwazi (meaning knowledge)
Tracker

Mama Unahti (meaning 'She is with us')
Kitchen manager

Simoshile (meaning beautiful feeling)
Teenage friend, Lwazi's daughter

André
Teenage friend

Zulu – English wordlist

Angiphili neze I am not feeling well
Eish! Oh dear!
Ibululu Puff adder
Iklwa Short stabbing spear, assegai
Isigubhu Drum
Izolo Yesterday
Kusasa Tomorrow
Namhlanje Today
Ngiyabonga Thank you
Ngiyakwemukela Welcome
Ngiyazi I know
Phuthuma Hurry up!
Sala khale Keep well
Sanibona Hallo (a group)
Sawubona Hallo (one person)
Suka Move / Go away
Thokoleza ukudla Enjoy your meal
Umfana Lad
Ungakhathazeki Never mind
Unjani How are you?
uNkulunkulu (or Ukulunkulu) Sky God

Street language / slang

Tsotsi Criminal or thug

Afrikaans – English wordlist

Beskuit Baked and oven-dried dough, cut to almost finger lengths. It is mostly flavoured with aniseeds, sour milk, or whole grain wheat and dried fruit, like raisins
Boomslang Directly translated as 'tree snake'
Engelsman Englishman
Foefieslide Flying fox / zip line
Kom Come
Swempie Coqui francolin

CHAPTER 1

There was blood on my fists. And blood on the boy's face. His name was Jonathan. A crowd had gathered around us in the school hallway. Jonathan lay there on the floor, looking up at me. His eyes still challenged me. He smiled as he wiped the blood away from his eye.

'Lucky shot!' he said.

'You want some more then?' In an instant my mind replayed the blow that floored Jonathan. The tension in my muscles. Teeth grinding. Eyes meeting eyes for only a moment. The pain shooting through my fist and up my arm as the blow hit home.

The crowd around us was like a pack of hyenas, hungry for more.

And then the teacher came.

There was trouble in the air. I just knew it. For days now I could feel it. It pushed up through the cold, wet streets. I breathed it in everywhere I went: the crowded trains in the London Underground, school classrooms, the newsstand on the corner, up through the streets. It had been going on for weeks now. And it made me scared.

It was late in the afternoon. Friday. I took the escalator and finally stepped out of the musty underground tunnels. Behind me I could still hear the echo of the underground railway and a busker playing the saxophone. The morning rain lined the streets. Specs of light from shop windows reflected on the wet pavement. Like scattered diamonds under the soles of the passers-by. I could hear their footsteps and suddenly wondered if they could hear mine. I wondered if they even listened. I wondered if they even cared.

Of course not, it was Friday. They all wanted to get home as soon as possible. Grey clouds covered the city. It would rain again very soon.

Trouble, I thought again.

There was trouble in the air.

The gripping fear made me quicken my pace. I tried finding comfort in the warmth of my jacket; in the familiar surroundings, the graffiti-covered walls. But the uneasy feeling followed me still. It hunted me like an animal.

I caught a sudden glimpse of my reflection in a shop window. Black face, fearful eyes, jaws clenched with cold. The cut on my lip.

And I felt like a stranger.

How could this be? I had lived in London all my life. I lived here with my mum in a two-bedroomed council flat above the street. I went to a state school here.

But somehow I was a stranger.

Was that what was bothering me?

Buyisiwe. My name echoed in my head. A stranger's name. Why not James, Chris or Peter? Or even Jonathan for that matter? Why not any other name, like most of the boys in school?

Buyisiwe. That is what they called me.

A Zulu name that meant: returned.

The rain was coming down in drifts as I got within a block of our flat. I hurried home. My clothes were cold and wet when I reached the front door. Determined to leave my fear outside, I breathed out forcefully. I stepped inside without glancing back.

Inside it felt warm. Safe.

I pushed back my cap and took the stairs to the second floor.

Shouting voices came from one of the flats. I ignored it like I always did. It would die down in a while anyway. But not before there'd been a banging of doors and maybe breaking glass. I didn't know any of the people living around us. I saw their faces every now and again. But I didn't know their names.

They certainly didn't know mine.

They didn't care, and neither did I.

Mum wasn't home yet. I switched on the TV on my way to the kitchen. The cartoon sounds of Tom and Jerry drowned out the world. In the kitchen I gulped down some milk straight from the carton. If my mum could see me now . . .

'How many times do I have to tell you to use a glass?'

That's what she would say.

Sometimes I do it just to piss her off.

There was some leftover pizza in the fridge. The cheese had turned an unappetising dull yellow in a sea of scattered bits of olive, pineapple and some sort of meat. I heated it in the microwave and went back into the living room. I made myself comfortable on the couch. Images flashed by on the TV screen. I didn't really take any notice. My mind drifted back to the fight I'd had at school. I tried telling myself that Jonathan deserved everything he'd got.

'Zulu!' his voice still rang in my ear. 'What are you doing here, Zulu? Why don't you go live with your people?'

Your people.

This was my home. I didn't know any other place.

I changed the TV channels and got up to fetch the pizza.

Somehow I knew that Jonathan's words weren't the only thing bothering me that day. There was something else: a hurried conversation Mum had had with me that morning.

'We have to have a talk,' she'd said.

'Not now, I'm late.'

'It's important, Buyi.'

'Mum!'

'Tonight then. When I get back from work.'

I knew something was troubling her too. It had been for more than a month now. I didn't want to ask her about it. I knew she would tell me when she was ready.

Trouble, said a voice from the back of my mind.

Trouble was brewing. And it wasn't something I could simply lock out. The trouble was already inside the flat.

CHAPTER 2

Mum sighed as she came in through the front door. Her eyes had dark rings under them; the rest of her face was paler than usual. Her blonde hair was in a mess, her clothes wrinkled. She tried to keep the door open with her foot, as she had shopping bags in one hand and a pizza box in the other.

'Well, don't just lie there, Buyi, come help me.'

'What? Pizza again?' I complained as I got up from the couch. 'We had pizza last night.'

'I'm tired. I'm not going to cook. Besides, you like pizza.'

'Yeah, but not every day.' I dropped the box on the kitchen counter and helped Mum with the bags.

'You could have cleaned up a bit, you know.' My eyes scanned the piles of dirty dishes, Coke-splattered counter top, overflowing dustbin. And the rest of the flat didn't look any better.

'I'm also tired. It's Friday. Who works on a Friday evening?'

'People who don't want to have rats and filthy cockroaches running amuck.'

'You can clean up tomorrow.'

'I have to work tomorrow!'

'Sunday then.'

Mum sighed and wiped her hands over her face. When she dropped her arms to her sides, there were tears welling up in her eyes. She leaned against the counter. 'You don't make life any easier for me, you know, Buyisiwe.'

'It's just rubbish, nothing to get excited over.'

'It's more than that. You don't help out at all around the house. I really struggle to keep food on the table, a roof over our heads. Do you know how tired I am of it all? But I can see now that I've made the right decision.'

'What decision?' The fear returned. I had seen my mum tired before, but something was different. There was a tone in her voice that I had never heard before. It was like she had given up. She was like an animal trapped in a cage, trying desperately to get out.

'I tried to tell you this morning, but you were in such a hurry. So, I let it go. I thought: let me think it over for another day. And then make my decision.'

Mum turned away. Tears were streaming down her face now. Her shoulders were shaking. I wanted to put my arms around her, but couldn't. Somehow there was a wall between us.

'You know I don't make rash decisions. I mull things over and over . . . And this time it hasn't been easy. It is probably the most difficult decision I have ever made.'

'Mum?' I now whispered.

'The thing that happened at school today, just confirmed everything. It was like a sign.'

'So, you found out about it?'

'The school phoned me, Buyi.' Mum wiped away the tears. She tilted her head slightly. Her face was sad. 'Mrs Fletcher told me about the fight. Apparently it wasn't the first one you've had. My heart sank when I heard about it, Buyi. Mrs Fletcher was adamant that she's had enough. And now I know that the time has finally come. I can't keep up supporting two people on my small salary. I've tried, and you know it.'

Mum fell silent for a moment. I could feel my world starting to spin around me. Things were about to change, I knew it. So this was it, I thought. This was the thing that had been following me around like a shadow. It was finally going to show its face.

'You are fourteen now, Buyi.' Mum almost whispered now. 'It is time for you to meet your father. Themba. I've phoned him a couple of times over the past month. I told him about our financial difficulties. We talked things over . . .'

'Mum?'

'Wait, Buyi, let me finish. I know he hasn't been there for you as you were growing up. But that will change now. He . . . he has agreed to look after you from now on.'

'What?' I cried. Terror filled my voice.

Mum nodded. 'Buyi, you're going to live with your father in South Africa.'

CHAPTER 3

I couldn't sleep for days after my talk with Mum. Her words kept haunting me: 'You're going to live with your father in South Africa.'

Every time I thought about it, my stomach churned. Africa? Where the hell is Africa anyway? Why do I have to go to Africa? Just because I got into a fight? For not fitting in? For being different?

I tried getting out of it, but Mum seemed to have thought it through carefully.

'You know I love you, Buyi, but it would be best for both of us now. When things take a turn for the better, we could discuss it again. Besides, you would like to meet your dad, wouldn't you?'

I really didn't know if I wanted to. She'd talked about him once or twice as I was growing up, but I'd never paid any attention. Where'd he been so far? He didn't care about me, or else he would have phoned or emailed. That's if they even have computers in Africa.

He didn't ask for pictures of me growing up. He didn't even send me gifts on my birthdays.

Why would I suddenly like to meet this man who has been ignoring me all of his life?

Following our discussion I often heard Mum talking to Themba, my so-called dad, on the phone.

Once she even held the handset out to me: 'Do you want to say hallo to your dad?'

I turned my back on her.

But I couldn't do it forever.

Mum had planned everything. She arranged my passport, got my father to pay for the ticket, packed my bags and off we went to Heathrow airport.

'You look scared,' said Mum. 'Don't be, please Buyi. It will turn out all right, you'll see. You'll love it, I'm sure. I'll phone.'

'When?'

'As soon as you get there.'

Here, and there. London and Johannesburg.

I didn't really have friends here, but if I had I wondered how they would have felt. It is not easy leaving everything you know behind. It is not easy packing up and simply going to live in another country.

South Africa, I thought, what would it be like living there? I have seen bits on television. Not much, though. It's the place where Nelson Mandela comes from. And they've got lots of wild animals down there. Would they be walking the streets? Do they even have streets and shopping malls? Do people over there live like people in London?

I'm sure I could have found loads of information on the Internet. But that would somehow have made leaving London all too real.

It couldn't have been more real than saying goodbye though.

'I love you, Mum,' I said, before I had to enter the departure hall. I don't think I had actually said it before and really meant it like that.

'And I love you, Buyi,' she said as she took me in her arms and hugged me. I wished I could have stayed there forever. But the time had come to leave.

'Come visit. Please!' I am sure it sounded like a cry for help, but I didn't care. Tears welled up in Mum's eyes. I wiped them away with my fingers. We both tried putting on a brave face but we couldn't.

And later when the plane took off, all I could think about was Mum, returning to an empty flat. Crying.

———

It was an eleven hour flight. The man sitting next to me was reading a newspaper. He had already been through it twice, and was busy with the third attempt. I caught glimpses of the headlines, but it didn't interest me. Neither did the movies they were showing. Around me I heard the voices of the other passengers. Strange languages. What language would they speak in South Africa, I wondered. This scared me. What if they didn't speak English! I didn't know any African languages.

My worry was soon replaced by another. The plane began to shake heavily.

'Ladies and gentleman,' announced the captain, 'we are entering an area of turbulence. It will only last for a few minutes, but we request that you fasten your seatbelts.'

My seatbelt was still fastened from our take-off. My eyes caught the white paper bag in the seat pocket in front of me. What would it feel like throwing up in an aeroplane miles above the Atlantic Ocean? Would the boring old man next to me even look up from his newspaper?

All the passengers fell silent. The plane shuddered heavily at times. And occasionally suddenly dropped. I closed my eyes but somehow it felt worse. I opened them again. *Lifejacket under your seat* were the first words I read on the tray table in front of me. I hoped it wasn't a sign of worse things to come. My mind flashed back to the emergency procedures given at the start of the journey. I looked around for the nearest exit sign. Again I noticed the lights on the floor. They didn't really look like lights; more like strips of plastic.

Before I could start imagining myself floating in a lifejacket in the ocean, the turbulence stopped.

The seatbelt sign was switched off. A few women rushed to the toilets. The air-hostesses continued serving drinks and snacks.

All was back to normal again.

I decided to get some rest. Leaning back in the chair I closed my eyes and dreamt of London.

CHAPTER 4

'Ladies and gentlemen, we are getting ready to land at O.R. Tambo International Airport,' announced the air-hostess. 'Please ensure that your tray tables are stowed, that all laptops and electronic devices are switched off and that your seatbelt is fastened.'

This was it. The moment I had been dreading. There was no turning back now. The air-hostesses strolled by, helping passengers, removing cushions and blankets, cups and glasses. Smiling. They really smiled a lot, these people. But of course they knew what to expect when we landed. I didn't. And I didn't feel like smiling either.

Nervously I glanced out the small window. The plane had descended below the clouds. The city of Johannesburg lay stretched out beneath us. Grey, dotted with splashes of green. Buildings as far as the eye could see, but it was different from London. There were tall buildings, but not really many skyscrapers. As we dropped even lower I began to see more clearly: trees, houses, patches of bright blue that could only be swimming pools. Lots of swimming pools. And cars. Thousands of them bustling down highways. And within moments the scenery below us changed. The large houses were replaced by suburbs with smaller houses. Grey, with silver roofs. Then again it changed to a large piece of land dotted with tiny shacks. Roughly constructed boxlike structures that had poverty written all over them.

I held my breath. And I thought we had it bad in London.

We approached the ground quickly now. Airport buildings, airplanes and landing strips flashed by. I was pushed back in my chair, feeling the force of the enormous engines. Then there was a slight bump: the wheels touching the runway.

I sighed softly as the runway and hundreds of small lights whizzed by. The wing flaps were pulled up, breaking our tremendous speed. Engines roared. The plane slowed down more and more. Eventually it reached a mere cruising speed as it taxied its way to the airport buildings.

Around me people started talking again, excitedly. I kept quiet. Just watching. Waiting for the plane to come to a complete stop.

Minutes later the passengers bustled out. I followed the stream of people.

And as my feet touched ground on African soil, I expected to feel a sudden jolt. A familiar connection, perhaps even a feeling of coming home to the land of my father.

But there was nothing.

I knew in an instant that I didn't belong there either.

We stood in line to get our passports checked and cleared. The man behind the counter looked solemn. He glanced over my passport and stamped it without hesitation.

I had a backpack over my shoulder but needed to get the rest of my luggage. Most people, it seemed, knew their way around the airport. I had to go on a hunch, keeping an eye out for signs or just following the other passengers like a lost sheep.

The bags made their way down the conveyor belt. At first I panicked when I saw only the one, but soon the other one appeared as well. Two bags filled to the brim with all my stuff. Or some of my stuff: I couldn't pack everything. Mum promised to keep the rest safe; said it would give her something to remember me by. I am sure a photograph would have been enough, but I knew she was right. I couldn't bring along the whole bloody room.

I needed a trolley, I now realized. I left the bags standing there and went off in search of one. When I arrived back, there was a man standing alongside my bags. He looked down at them, then at me.

'Are these yours?'

'Yes.' I looked at him, and then at his uniform. He was with airport security.

'You shouldn't leave them around,' he said. 'Someone might take them.'

'I was just gone for a minute.'

'That's more than enough time for them to disappear.'

I nodded, but wondered who would want to take my bags?

'Are you South African?'

'No.'

'I thought so,' he nodded. A smile appeared on his face. 'If you have anything to declare, you have to go to Customs. Let me help you with those bags.'

'I'll manage,' I said, but he had already taken one of my bags and lifted it onto the trolley. I placed the second one on. My backpack too.

'What's your name?'

Why does this stranger want to know my name? I asked myself. I answered none the less. 'Buyisiwe.'

'Returned,' he said, and then frowned. 'I thought you said you're not from around here.'

'I'm not,' I said as I walked away.

'Good luck then!' he shouted. 'I have a feeling you're going to need it, Buyisiwe.'

I hoped he was wrong about that. His words didn't put my mind at ease at all. I was suddenly very conscious of all that was going on around me. The announcements being made inside the terminal building, the expressions of the people scurrying about: some rigid, confused, happy, relaxed, angry. The slightly musty smell of baggage mixing with floor polish.

As I stepped into the arrivals hall I was met with a sea of expectant faces. People waiting for their loved ones, tour operators awaiting their customers, chauffeur services waiting for business men.

Who would be there waiting for me?

'Your dad will pick you up.' That is what Mum had said.

I didn't know what he looked like. I had only seen his face once on a faded picture. The picture I had of him in my mind had faded even further by now.

My gaze drifted across all the people. My heart began thumping. My mouth was dry.

What if he hadn't come? It was a scary thought. I would be left there all alone. More alone than I had ever been in my life.

Then a sign caught my eye. It had my name on it. Buyisiwe.

The man carrying it looked around worriedly. He was dressed in a neat khaki uniform and leather shoes. As soon as his eyes met mine, he smiled. Rows of pearly white teeth showing up against his kind black face.

My dad had come for me. The relief washed over me.

So, this was him. This was Themba.

CHAPTER 5

'Sawubona!' the man called, holding out his hand to me. 'Ngiyakwemukela!'

I frowned. I had no idea what he'd said. 'Sorry?'

'I said *Hallo, welcome!*' He laughed and again his smile spread across his face.

'Uh hi, thanks,' I answered apprehensively. My heart was still racing. Somehow, meeting your father for the first time is a mind-blowing experience. Not mind-blowingly good, mind-blowingly terrifying.

His hand was still stretched out towards me. I took it, his grip soft. Then he did a strange thing, shifting his hand from a normal handshake to gripping my thumb, again gently, and back to a normal handshake.

'Oh,' I said, taken aback.

'Sawubona!' he said again.

I nodded sheepishly. 'You're Themba, right? My dad?' I don't know why I said it. The words just came spilling out. Of course he was my father.

'No!' the man said loudly, 'I'm Lwazi. I work with your dad.'

What? The unsettled feeling inside me increased. 'But where's my dad then?'

'He still had some work to do, so he asked me to come and pick you up.'

'But my mum said Themba will –'

'Don't worry, I'll look after you.' Lwazi smiled again, patting me on the shoulder. I didn't like that at all. After all I'd been through I would have expected my dad to come and fetch me himself. Could I even trust this guy? He seemed friendly enough, but you never know. I didn't like strangers. It was just the way I had been brought up. Living in a big city like London also did that to you.

I glanced around the arrivals hall, trying to see if the security officer who had talked to me earlier was still around. If there were any problems, I could call him. He was nowhere to be seen but there were others around now, also dressed in uniforms. Hopefully there were some in plain clothes as well.

'Let me help you with your baggage,' Lwazi offered.

'No!' I snapped, grabbing the trolley. The conversation I'd had only minutes ago with the security officer was still fresh in my mind.

'You're afraid,' said Lwazi.

'I'm . . . I'm careful.'

'That is always a good thing. Especially in South Africa.'

Yes, I was afraid of all of this, but I was trying to hide my fear. Arriving in a strange new country that you are supposed to call your home from now on; then barely having set foot in the country and getting warned about being robbed; and having a total stranger pick you up at the airport. That would make anyone apprehensive.

'You're here!' I heard somebody calling.

'Buyisiwe!'

A white boy and a black girl came running. They were about my age. Fourteen. They too were smiling, their faces lighting up as if they had known me all their lives. I stepped back as they approached.

'Sorry we missed you,' said the freckle-faced boy with the red hair. 'Simoshile had to go to the ladies. And I had to see that she didn't get lost. She's got no sense of direction at all.'

The girl's eyes widened. 'André! Shut up!'

The boy shook my hand and placed his arm around my shoulder. It felt strange to me. Should I just shrug it off, or would it be rude to do that?

'My name is André,' he said excitedly.

The girl smiled gently. Her dark brown eyes were kind as she introduced herself: 'And I'm Simoshile.'

'Buyisiwe,' I said, but then remembered that they already knew it. After all, they'd called my name as they came running.

'I see you've met Lwazi,' said André.

'I think Buyi thought I was a tsotsi!' laughed Lwazi. 'A criminal.'

'If there is one person you can trust completely, it is Lwazi,' said André. 'I'm not so sure about Simoshile, though.' Simoshile's eyebrows rose suddenly. André's eyes twinkled mischievously as he added, 'She just might steal your heart!'

Simoshile gave André a shove. He laughed playfully, winking at me.

'I'll get you for that, André!' said Simoshile.

'Enough of this fooling around,' said Lwazi as he took hold of my trolley. This time I let him, feeling much more at ease. 'I'm sure Buyi is tired. We have to get going. There is still a long road ahead.'

Exactly where this long road would take me, I only found out much later.

CHAPTER 6

Outside the airport terminal Lwazi stopped for a moment and looked around, trying to find his way. I reckoned he didn't come there often. But he wasn't lost. Within seconds he had his wits about him and headed for a parking garage.

'Aren't we going to take the Underground?' I asked.

'The what?' frowned André. Simoshile looked questioningly at Lwazi. She didn't know what I was talking about either. Lwazi shrugged.

'The train. The underground train.'

'Oh that!' said Lwazi. 'There isn't one.'

How could it be? I wondered. From the air Johannesburg seemed like such a big and bustling city, surely they would need an underground rail system.

Then Lwazi added, 'Not at the moment. But they are busy building one right now. They call it the Gautrain. You are now in the province of Gauteng. So, the train would be named after the province.'

'So people just drive to wherever they want to be?' I asked.

'No,' answered Lwazi. 'There are trains of course, but they run above ground. And if you have to travel very far, you could catch a plane. Lots of people get around in their cars or in taxis. You will soon see them.'

Lwazi paid at a parking station, and we headed for the car.

I saw Simoshile stealing quick glances in my direction every now and again. Was something wrong? I looked down to make sure my fly was done up. It was. I shook my head. It was probably nothing.

André talked a lot. He spoke English with a strange accent.

'I'm Afrikaans,' explained André. 'It is my home language. But I speak English as well. And a little bit of isiZulu. Not much though, just enough to get me into trouble,' he grinned.

Three languages! How is that possible?

'That's nothing,' said Simoshile. 'I speak isiZulu and English. And bits of Afrikaans, isiXhosa and siSwati.' She too had a strange accent, but it differed from André's.

'How many languages do you have in South Africa?' I asked.

'Eleven official languages,' said Simoshile before André could answer.

'Show off,' was all he managed to get out.

I only spoke English. How could these people get by with so many languages without getting totally confused? No wonder they all had these strange accents. Come to think of it, my English probably sounded strange to them as well.

We reached the car. It was a 4x4 off-road vehicle with twin cabs. Lwazi packed my suitcases in the back of the vehicle. André and I got in on the backseat. Simoshile jumped in at the front next to Lwazi.

As Lwazi started the vehicle, I felt a tiredness washing over me. There was still a distant fear lingering somewhere within me. Fear of the unknown. But there was also a faint spark of excitement. In the coming days I would learn that this excitement was to burn brightly at times. But there would be other times when it was to fade away completely.

We made our way out of the airport grounds and were immediately caught up in the bustle of Johannesburg's hectic traffic. They too drove on the left side of the road, like we do in England. Some of the people around us drove like madmen. Huge trucks slowed down the traffic. Most of them kept to the left lanes, while other cars overtook on the right.

I read the road signs. We were on the Pretoria road. All around the highway there were businesses, factories and what Simoshile called 'townhouse complexes'. This was where people lived in apartments of varying sizes, with the whole complex surrounded by security walls topped with electric fences.

I soon realized that these people were crazy about security. They had security cameras, fences, walls, security guards, burglar-proofing on all windows, security gates, security doors and alarms.

Shocking!

I thought back to the flat windows in London that would be boxed with metal frames and mesh iron when it was left unoccupied. That kept people from breaking in, but what I saw in Johannesburg was a hundred times worse.

It was as if they had built themselves these little prisons to live in.

Minibus taxis whizzed by us on the highway. They were almost always overcrowded with nine or more occupants. They didn't seem to care much for the rules of the road.

We were driving north, I think. We kept on the road they called the N1, passing through a toll once. Then the scenery changed suddenly. The buildings fell away. There were more open spaces around us, dotted with trees and covered in grasslands. Again some buildings appeared, then a place that made my throat tighten.

'It's a squatter camp,' said Simoshile, pointing to the dilapidated shacks. I had seen something similar from the air as we were about to land. And now I was right next to one. The shacks were built with zinc metal sheets and pieces of wood. In places there was plastic covering small windows. Some shacks didn't even have windows. Roofs were kept down with rocks. From where I was sitting it seemed terrible. How could people live in these conditions every day?

The children playing around the ramshackle houses seemed happy though. Their faces were dirty, their clothes worn, but they were happy as only kids can be. Was it because they didn't know any better?

Why was it so filthy and overcrowded? Why did people allow this to happen?

Then a thought suddenly struck me: I still didn't know where exactly we were heading. What if I was about to be dropped off here? What if my dad lived here in one of these shacks? It was a terrifying thought.

Silently I prayed that the car wouldn't stop here or even slow down slightly. *Drive on! Just drive on!* a voice screamed inside me.

We drove past the squatter camp. I felt terribly ashamed. I realized I had stared into the bleak face of poverty. And I wanted nothing to do with it. Little did I realize that I was not the only one. The world was full of people just like me. People who didn't give a damn about things like this just because they didn't have to stare it in the face every day.

CHAPTER 7

Before I realised it I had fallen asleep. It had been a tiring day and I just couldn't keep my eyes open any longer. With the soft drone of the 4x4's engine in my ears, I dreamt of living in a place where I felt at home. All the tension of the last few hours faded away.

It was already late afternoon when I woke up. The sun was shining in my face. I heard voices. André and Simoshile were bickering over something.

'Ah, look! The sleeping princess has woken!' said André teasingly, turning his head my way. 'And just in time too. I was about to get something to drink. You want anything?'

I stared around. We were in a small town, at a shopping centre, built almost in a U-shape. Cars were parked all around in the middle. 'I'll go with you,' I said, yawning. 'I need to stretch my legs.'

'Then I'm coming too,' said Simoshile, jumping out of the vehicle.

'Don't take too long,' said Lwazi, as he headed in another direction. 'I just need to get some things for Mama Unahti's kitchen. Be back in fifteen minutes!'

The town was called Bela-Bela.

'It's famous for the hot springs in the town centre,' said André. 'Just a place for a bunch of old ladies to hang about gossiping, if you ask me,' he added. Until very recently Bela-Bela had apparently been called Warmbaths.

We entered the store. It was way smaller than the Tesco I was used to. The products on the shelves were also different. But one surely wasn't . . .

'Coke okay for you?' asked André, already standing at the opened refrigerator door.

I nodded, enjoying the fleeting coolness wafting out of the fridge. The South African summers were a lot hotter than those in London.

André bought himself a magazine called NAG. It had topics ranging from games and computers to new technology. I watched him handing the money over to the cashier. That was another thing I would have to get used to: a new currency. Rand. The four cans of Coke and the magazine came to R67.96. That's a little over £6, I worked out in my head.

We were soon back on the road. Another half hour drive took us to a dirt road branching off from the tarmac road.

Now I knew why they needed an off-road vehicle. We bumped around, heading on, but it didn't seem to bother the others.

'Do you see there?' asked André, pointing to a mountain range in the distance. I nodded. 'It's the Waterberg Mountains.' I stared at the solid-looking green and brown mountain, its jagged edges cutting across the sky.

A further fifteen minute drive brought us to a magnificent wooden gate, winged by a stone wall stretching out to the sides. A sign read: Isigubhu. And below it in smaller letters: Drum.

A uniformed security guard opened the gate. He obviously knew Lwazi, André and Simoshile. He waved us through, smiling.

'Ngiyabonga!' shouted Lwazi through his opened window. It probably meant 'thank you'. But I wasn't too sure. The guard nodded and lifted his hand.

We drove on a bit further. There was an incessant buzz in the air. I didn't know what it was but it seemed to come from the trees or the grass or somewhere. André and Simoshile didn't seem to notice it at all.

We eventually reached a cluster of stone buildings with high thatched roofs set off against the backdrop of the Waterberg Mountains. The main building was simple but quite impressive. It had large windows and huge wooden doors covered with intricately carved animals. Flanking the spacious, tiled veranda were over-sized clay pots with water spilling over the edges. Two other buildings flanked the larger one. A sign at the door of one of them read Curio Shop. The other one was a spa and beauty salon. The buildings were all interlinked by a magnificent garden filled with flowers. The cool green of the trees looked inviting. I was suddenly reminded of the parks in London. But this garden was somehow different, more natural and earthly.

'Welcome to your new home!' said Lwazi as he parked in the shade near the main building.

'What is this place?' I asked.

'Don't you know?' he smiled. 'It's a game reserve.'

'Is this where I'm going to live?'

'Well, not in here exactly. You might get in the way of all the tourists passing through. You'll stay at your dad's chalet in the employee part of the resort. It is a bit further down the road. More private.'

My mind started racing again. I'm going to live in a game reserve. Was that a good or a bad thing? I didn't really know. I looked around to see if there were any animals around. Should I be afraid? I hadn't had much contact with animals. A cat or a dog here and there. Perhaps a bird. But I'd never had one of my own.

Animals. Wild animals.

Yeah, that was something to be scared of, of course! And I'm going to live here . . .

Mum never said anything about animals. Did she want to keep it as a surprise?

André and Simoshile jumped out of the vehicle. They seemed quite at ease. Not afraid at all.

'Do you like it?' asked André.

'Of course he does!' said Simoshile.

I nodded, trying to look brave, but I was scared as hell. I'd seen the Discovery Channel. I knew what wild animals could do. I'd probably need a cricket bat or some kind of weapon to protect me, should some wild thing come charging from the bushes.

Bushes!

There were lots of bushes around. And trees. Animals could be hiding anywhere.

'This place is the best!' said André.

Simoshile must have sensed my apprehension. 'Hey, it will be all right. You'll see.' Her voice was soft and calm. 'You don't have to be afraid.'

As soon as she said that, I felt calmness slowly washing over me. I guess she was right. Perhaps I was just being silly.

'Oh! Is he here?' I heard somebody cry. A large woman with a colourful animal-print dress and matching headscarf came storming out of the building and down the steps. Her arms were outstretched, fingers spread wide and palms open. 'My boy! My boy!' she cried. Her whole body seemed to shiver with excitement. Her eyes wide and lively, a smile as big as a sickle moon.

Before I knew it, she grabbed me, first by the shoulders saying, 'Let me look at you!' Then she pulled me closer to her more than generous bosom, enveloping me totally. She had a sweet smell, as if the scent of the flowers in the garden had rubbed off on her.

'Unjani? Unjani?' she hummed. 'How are you?'

I was totally taken aback. I stood there in her embrace, not knowing what to do. Who was this woman? Am I supposed to know her? What should I do? Hug her back?

'Welcome home, Buyisiwe,' she said. 'You have returned at last.'

'Um, hallo,' was all I could manage to say when she let go of me.

'My name is Unahti, but everyone calls me Mama,' she said proudly.

'Mama Unahti runs the kitchen,' said Simoshile, giving her a hug.

'And everything else as well if you give her half a chance!' teased André.

'Hey suka!' she cried, pretending to be cross but seemingly loving it. 'Don't pay any attention to this naughty boy, Buyi. He'll just get you into trouble.'

'But Mama would get me out of trouble again. She always does,' said André.

She smiled as she rolled her eyes, then her gaze once again fixed on me. 'Oh you're so sweet, Buyi! I could just eat you!' she cried again, pinching my cheek.

I was glad none of the bullies at my old school were here to witness all this. I could just imagine myself becoming the butt of every joke. There's Buyi. He's so sweet, you could just eat him!

That was sure to get your ass kicked a few times.

'Let's get you something to eat, Buyi. Are you hungry?'

'Yeah, starving.'

'I thought so. I made some lovely – '

But Mama Unahti didn't get to finish her sentence. Just as we were about to head up the steps to the main building, we heard a car approaching.

Or rather, it was another off-road vehicle. Green, with dusty tyres. At the open back there were a number of seats, all filled with exhausted looking people. Tourists, it seemed. Two blackmen were sitting at the front.

'Oh, look,' said Mama Unahti. 'Your dad is here.'

CHAPTER 8

It was the strangest feeling, meeting my dad for the second time. Okay, the first time it wasn't really him, it was Lwazi. But now there was no mistaking it anymore. My stomach churned. I felt jittery. From the look on the driver's face I knew it was him: Themba.

He looked smart in his khaki uniform. The long-sleeved shirt rolled up over his muscled forearms. Leather shoes and wide brimmed hat. His face was strong, square jaw, dark eyes. We looked very much alike.

He must have noticed me standing there. He nodded from afar in my direction as he helped the tourists off the vehicle. His eyes continuously darted back to me.

Should I run up to him, and hug him like Mama had hugged me? Or should I wait for him to approach me?

When the tourists started chattering amongst themselves, looking at each other's digital photos on their cameras, Themba excused himself. As he approached, my heart beat faster and faster. This was the first time I would ever see him up-close in real life. He was part of me, but I didn't know him at all. He was as much of a stranger as all the people I had met that day: Lwazi, André, Simoshile, and Mama Unahti.

But this stranger's life was connected to mine. He was my father.

With his hat in his hand he stood before me. Looking at me. He blinked once, twice. His face taut.

I felt my mouth go dry. I didn't know what to expect from him. I made myself ready for an embrace like the one Mama gave me. But it didn't come. He just held out his hand and in a strong voice said, 'Hallo, Buyisiwe.' That was all. No hugs. No smile. Just a distant hallo. I shook his hand like Lwazi did with me earlier. Shake, thumb, shake.

'Hi.' Should I call him Dad? Or Themba? 'Themba . . .'

He didn't correct me, so I guess it was okay with him.

Mama Unahti must have sensed the uneasy tension between us. With a loud voice she called, 'I was just about to get the boy something to eat. Why don't you join him, Themba? You two must have loads to talk about.'

'I can't right now, Unahti. I have to see to the guests.' His eyes darted back to mine, void of emotion.

Was he at all glad to see me?

'You'll be okay won't you, Buyisiwe? I'll see you later.' He dug in his pocket and removed a key. 'This will let you into the chalet. Lwazi will take you. It's not far. You can actually walk there, but you probably have some baggage?' I nodded. 'Good . . . well then . . .'

With that he turned around and made his way back to the guests. Their excitement had still not died down. I could hear their laughter ringing, even as we stepped into the building.

Mama Unahti gently placed her hand around my shoulder. 'I've got some mouth-watering dessert, too,' she said.

I tried not to think about the hurt surging inside me.

Mama Unahti, I soon found out, believed that all sorrows can be drowned out by food. I was so stuffed when Lwazi finally dropped me off at my dad's chalet.

I stood at the front door for a moment, looking around. It was a neat, brick building with a thatched roof. To the side there was a brick wall encircling what looked like an entertainment area with some tables, chairs and a fireplace. There was no garden. If it wasn't for the narrow cement slab and a small clearing running around the building, the bush would have almost reached right up to the chalet. Only some trees were left standing in the clearing, their cool shade falling across the brown earth.

Lwazi helped me with the baggage. I unlocked the front door. As I stepped inside the mellow scent of the thatched roof stopped me in my tracks for a moment. I looked around. This was my new home. Two bedrooms, a kitchen, bathroom and a sitting area right in the centre of it all. The place was immaculately clean. Nothing like the place where Mum and I lived. Against one of the walls the head of a dead animal glared down at me. Its black eyes sent a shiver down my back. It was some sort of antelope. Towering horns curling up to the ceiling.

'I think this might be your room,' said Lwazi. He carried my suitcases inside.

I followed him. The room was spacious enough. I opened the closet. It was bare, with ample place for my clothes and stuff. A small desk and chair stood against the wall. I tested the single bed standing near the window. It felt comfortable, as did the two pillows.

'You seem right at home!' smiled Lwazi. 'I have to get going. I'm joining André's dad, Johan, on a night safari. He's a game ranger just like your dad.'

'And you?' I asked.

'I'm a tracker.'

I frowned. 'Tracker?'

'I track animals. I go along looking for tracks, and other signs. It helps the ranger find the animals far more easily. The tourists find it exciting too. It is easy to get caught up in the tension of tracking an animal.'

I smiled half-heartedly. I couldn't imagine tracking animals being fun.

'Keep the windows closed, Buyi,' said Lwazi as he left. 'Baboons sometimes get nosy. They might rearrange the whole house for you if you're not careful. They'll eat anything they can lay their hands on. Even go rummaging through your fridge!'

What!

'And . . . and other animals? Will I be safe here on my own?'

'There's no need to worry. Animals are usually more afraid of you than you are of them. You might see some around. Perhaps an impala or two. Maybe even some warthogs. It is getting dark. That's the time some animals like to go out hunting or grazing. Especially if there's a full moon in the sky.'

With that he left, shouting, 'Sala khale!' over his shoulder. 'Keep well!'

I was suddenly all alone. Darkness was starting to creep into the house. I switched on all the lights, thankful that there was at least electricity here. I needed some noise. Noise! Or else I would go mad.

Switch on the TV. That always helps. Having the drone of voices and music around. Flickering images to keep you company.

I walked through the house a couple of times. I looked everywhere, even opening up some closets.

There was no TV!

This is insane, I thought. How could it be? Surely they must have heard of television before? Yes of course, there was one in the lounge at the main building. I'd noticed it in passing earlier, as I followed Mama Unahti. But none in the chalet. I'm going to die here, I thought. If not in the jaws of some wild animal, then from boredom.

No TV!

A sudden shrill sound shattered the silence around me. A telephone! I was so glad to hear that irritating ring that I ran right over and answered it.

'Hi there, Buyi!'

'Mum!' I was so relieved to hear a familiar voice.

'How are you?'

'I'm fine, I guess. And you?'

'Missing you, of course. The place feels so empty without you. How was the flight?'

We talked and talked. I told Mum about the trip here, everything I'd seen, the people I'd met.

'And how's your father? Are you getting along?'

'He's great,' I lied. I didn't want Mum to worry about me.

'Well then,' she said eventually, 'I probably have to say goodbye now. Love you, my boy.'

'Love you too, Mum,' I said, biting back the tears.

CHAPTER 9

I unpacked my bags. The clothes I stashed away in the cupboard, the few books I'd brought along I stacked on the desk, alongside a pack of CDs and DVDs. On the bare brick wall I stuck a poster of Amir Khan, the famous boxer. I stared up at him for a while, sighed softly and then continued getting the room comfortable.

The silence still lingered. All I heard was my own footsteps on the tile floor, the gentle rustle of my clothes as I moved about the room. I had never heard my clothes move. It felt strange.

Deep, deep silence.

I sat down on my bed, cross-legged. I tilted my head to the side. No, there were other sounds. They were coming from outside. Muffled. I glanced at the window on my left.

Should I open it for a short while? But what if something came leaping through it all of a sudden? Or swinging through it – the baboon Lwazi was talking about.

Oh, don't be so damn scared, I reprimanded myself.

I placed my hand on the window latch, turned it ever so carefully.

Click!

Slowly I opened the window. The sounds of the night came flooding into my room. There were crickets chirping. Birds calling. At least, I thought it was birds. I listened. Three or four different kinds of birds. I didn't know their names. Their shrill calls echoed through the night. On and on.

Ke-koik, ke koik!

Fu-eek, fu-eek, fu-eek!

Ke-teh-teh-teh-teh-teh!

A bug suddenly whirred through the window. I fell backwards on the bed, startled for a moment. The black-winged beetle flew up to the light. I had to smile. It had almost given me the fright of my life but it seemed innocent enough.

I sat upright at the window again, listening to the birds. Trying to recognize the strange smells wafting through the air. It had to be leaves, dry grass, dust.

It was pitch-dark outside. So dark that it seemed as if a black velvet curtain had been hung right on the other side of the window. Drowning out all light, but not the sounds or the smells.

Something scratched out there in the bush. I could hear the rustle of grass, the crackling of dry leaves and twigs.

It sounded like something heavy.

An animal?

My mind raced, trying to find an explanation. Should I close the window now? Perhaps it wasn't even near the chalet. I couldn't really judge its distance, my mind not being accustomed to something like this.

I listened again. It seemed quite near.

There were no animal sounds, just the continuous scratching and rustling. I probably would have swallowed my tongue if that animal were to suddenly call out. Or worse, jump up at the window!

Enough bravery for one night.

I closed the window, making doubly sure the latch was properly secured. I fell back on my bed, staring out into the dark. Wondering what Mum was up to now.

Themba still hadn't come home.

I must have fallen asleep there on the bed, still wearing the clothes I'd had on when I arrived. The bang of a door woke me up. Hasty footsteps. I lay there frozen, breathless. Something moved outside my door.

'Dammit!' It was a man's voice.

I heard him ruffling through a cupboard. The sound of metal. A safe opening? A clinking sound. The safe closing.

Again hurried footsteps moving away, stopping near the front door, returning. Approaching my room. A shadow fell across the doorway.

'Buyi, are you awake?' It was Themba.

'Yes . . .'

'I have to go out again. Ensure all the doors and windows are shut properly.' His voice was anguished. He looked tired, but he was obviously in a hurry.

'What's wrong?' Only now did I see the rifle in his hand. Shining ammunition in the other.

'There has been an accident. The night safari . . .'

'The one Lwazi went on?'

He nodded, his brow furrowing even more. 'They met with a lion.'

'Is he all right?'

'We don't know. The radio signal was too weak. I'm off to find them. Stay here.'

I nodded. The blood drained from my body, leaving me weak. As soon as I heard the front door slam, I ran through the chalet making sure every door that could be locked was locked. Every window latched.

Fear had set in. And I didn't like it at all.

I couldn't sleep anymore. I waited and waited for Themba to come home. Dreading every minute of it.

Hours later, I heard the scratching at the front door.

A lion, my mind cried.

No, I heard a key turning in the lock. The door swung open. Themba entered. His clothes were all covered in blood.

CHAPTER 10

'What happened?' I asked fearfully.

Themba sighed, shook his head wearily and went to his room to lock the rifle away in the safe.

'I'm going to take a shower,' he said. 'Why aren't you in bed?'

'I couldn't –'

'Get to your room!'

'You're all covered in blood! Are you okay?'

'Yes, now go!'

I wanted to scream with frustration. Who's blood was that? Did he kill the lion? Or had the lion . . . No, I didn't even want to think about that.

I heard the shower being turned on. Water rushing.

My dreams were restless, haunted with worry.

It started to rain sometime during the night. But by the time Themba got up it had cleared again. Five o' clock. What is he doing up that early, I wondered sleepily. I stayed in bed and listened to him moving about the house. He left without saying a word.

I must have dozed off again.

When I finally got up, I helped myself to an apple for breakfast. I found a hi-fi tucked away in a cabinet in a corner and put a CD on. Bloc Party. I got into the shower and jumped around under the water, dancing to one of the tracks. *Where is home?* always got me in a good mood.

As I got dressed I heard the excited voice of André outside the house. I went to open up the front door.

'Have you heard?' he said as he came bustling in. 'Simoshile's dad was bitten by a lion last night! Lwazi, you know?'

'Is Lwazi Simoshile's dad?' I asked, but then it struck me: that's not what caused André's excitement. 'Bitten by a lion?'

'Yeah, how cool is that!' André's bright blue eyes shone.

'Not cool at all . . . Is he all right?'

'He's fine. They took him to the hospital last night. He'll be back again later today. Knowing him, he'd rather have them cut off his arm than stay in hospital.'

'What happened?' I asked. 'I know Lwazi and your dad took some tourists on a night safari. And that they met with a lion. Themba went to help.'

'Their Land Rover got stuck in mud. My dad was still busy trying to get it out when Lwazi spotted this lone male lion wandering around the bush. He had the searchlight pinned on him. The people took photos and that's when it happened . . .'

'What?'

'I don't know anything further. I overheard Dad telling Mum all of this when he came back. He closed their bedroom door just as the story got exciting.'

'André!'

'Sorry, I also want to know what happened.'

'So the blood on Themba's clothes . . . it was Lwazi's?'

'Yeah, probably. I'm sure he bled a lot.'

At least I know something now, I thought.

'So, what are we doing today?' asked André.

'I'm staying right here,' I said. 'I'm not going out if there is a man-eating lion running about.'

'Jeez, you're weird,' grinned Andre. 'This game reserve is so big, what's the chance of you meeting up with him? Anyway, lions are most dangerous at night. By day they mostly laze about in the shadows of the candle-pod acacias. That's why they call it the House of the Lion.'

'I don't know . . .' I said hesitantly.

'I can't believe you're so scared.'

Still I hesitated.

'Come on, Buyi! Trust me, it's okay!'

'All right then.'

'We'll get something to eat first, in Mama's kitchen. Then off we'll go.'

Stepping outside the house I got a whiff of last night's rain. It mixed with the other spicy scents the bush conjured up. Walking back to the main building of the resort, André explained to me how the game reserve was divided up into three camps: Izolo, Namhlanje and Kusasa. Yesterday, today and tomorrow. The Big Five roamed about in two of them: Izolo and Namhlanje.

'That's the biggest African animals, right?' I tried to sound informed.

'Actually no,' said André. 'The Big Five is an old hunting term for the most dangerous animals to hunt: lions, leopards, elephants, buffalo and black rhinos.'

So much for my superior knowledge!

'And you have them all here?'

'Yip!'

'The other camp's animals are less dangerous. But you still have to be careful. Respect them, and they will respect you, that's what my dad always says.' André strode on fast. 'Oh, and you never know when you might come across an elephant in the Kusasa camp. There isn't much that would stop an elephant once he gets it into his head to wander across to the other side of the fence . . .'

My eyes must have widened, because André suddenly burst out laughing.

I couldn't tell if he was only teasing me, or not.

'My boys!' cried Mama Unahti, taking us in her arms in one great sweep. Hugging us.

André seemed to enjoy this. He was probably used to this by now. I still felt a bit uneasy. He grinned, sensing my discomfort.

'Have you had any breakfast yet?' she asked, her eyes fixed on us, expectantly. She had on a large, colourful dress again, this time decorated with geometric shapes.

'I had some at home,' smiled André, 'but I won't say no to a plate of your maize porridge. You know I'm always hungry.'

'Oh, you are growing up my boy, that's why!' Mama Unahti waved her hands through the air. 'And you, Buyi? Did your dad prepare you some breakfast this morning?'

'Uh . . . no, Mama.'

'What?'

'He went out very early. I . . . I had an apple, though.'

'An apple?' she cried, slamming her hands together. 'That is not enough! I'll have to talk to that man. He should know that he's got a responsibility now.' She seemed quite annoyed. 'Ungakhathazeki. Never mind.' She indicated for us to follow her. 'I've got some steamy porridge on the stove.'

Kitchen workers scattered about as Mama Unahti entered the kitchen. Some of them, I think, merely tried to look busy. Were they scared of this loving woman?

Yes!

'Why is this counter top so filthy?' she cried in a high voice. 'Clean up! Clean up! Put away that milk. It will turn sour in minutes in this heat.'

She moved through the kitchen, her eyes noticing every little thing. 'There are dirty dishes in the wash basin. Where's the dish washer? Is he having a smoke break again? I'll break something very precious of his if I see another dirty cup in my kitchen!

Hurry up! Phuthuma!'

Mama Unahti reached for two clean plates and spoons. There was a big silver pot on the stove. She opened the lid and clouds of steam billowed to the roof. Taking a large ladle, she scooped out two heaps of white stuff.

My eyes widened. 'What is that?'

'Ngiyabonga, Mama!' said André as he took the plate, his eyes gleaming.

'Gi-ya-bo-a' I tried. The sound was strange on my tongue, sounding quite stupid.

'Ah, the boy is starting to speak isiZulu!' cried Mama. All the kitchen helpers looked at me and cheered. Now I felt even more stupid.

'Ngi-ya-bon-ga!' said Mama, leaning over towards me and saying the word slowly.

'Ngi-ya-bon-ga!' I repeated.

'That's better! Thokoleza ukudla! That means *enjoy your meal.*'

'Tho-ko-leza u-kud-la . . .' I practised, as I followed André to the dining room.

I was still wondering how on earth I was going to eat this stuff Mama called porridge. André didn't seem to have that problem. He dropped a pat of butter on top of the porridge, then some sugar. As he watched it melt down into the warm porridge, I did the same. Later we added some fresh milk and mixed it all up.

My first bite . . . It was sweet and creamy. Almost sticky, but not quite. Full of flavour. Very strange, but good. I was surprised. Before I knew it my plate was empty. André had finished his too. We took the plates back to the kitchen.

'Ngiyabonga, Mama!' I said, seeing the satisfied look in her eyes.

CHAPTER 11

Simoshile was still with her dad at the hospital. Armed only with water bottles, André and I began strolling down the dust road. He knew the way, I just followed.

Like a shining balloon the sun was moving higher against the crisp blue sky. I could already feel its hot rays burning down, stinging my neck.

'Where do you go to school?' I asked André.

'Do we have to talk about that now?' he groaned. 'I'm trying hard to forget about the S word.'

'Okay,' I shrugged.

'It's holiday, I don't even want to think about school. Ah! There; you made me say the word!'

'Sorry,' I grinned.

'Might as well tell you now. We, that's Simoshile and I, attend school in Bela-Bela. It's a High School. We're in grade nine. A bus picks us up every morning and brings us back in the afternoon after sport practice.'

'Sport practice?'

'Rugby in winter and cricket or athletics in summer.'

'You play rugby?'

'Yes, I'm left wing. Fastest boy in our grade.' His eyes glimmered with pride. 'And you?'

'I don't like sport much. I like watching boxing. And soccer.'

'And what grade are you in?'

'In England we don't call it grades. I'm in year nine, which I guess is pretty much the same.'

'I can't wait to finish my Matric . . .' sighed André.

'Matric?' I asked.

'Last year of school.'

'Oh, we call it A levels.'

He nodded. His face suddenly lit up. 'I want to be a game ranger just like my dad. And you?'

'I don't know yet.'

'You'll have lots of time to think about it here, Engelsman.'

'Engelsman?' I frowned.

'Englishman,' he translated, smiling mischievously. I shook my head, smiling back.

We reached a huge gate made of iron and spanned with lengths of wire. A sign next to it read: Kusasa.

'This isn't the one with the lion, is it?' I asked carefully.

'Of course not,' said André, opening it. We slipped through. He closed it again behind us.

Ahead of us a dirt road wound its way through the trees, shrubs and grass. Easy enough, I thought, until André stepped off the road, and into the bush.

'Kom!' he said. It sounded like 'come'. I followed him. At places the ground was smooth, allowing us to march along without trouble, but at other places it was quite uneven. There were tufts of grass everywhere. Some sap-green, others dry and yellow. I kept my eyes on the ground, trying not to sprain an ankle.

'At the rate you're going I reckon a tortoise would overtake you,' said André. He stood ahead of me, hands at his sides. Waiting.

I quickened my pace.

All around us, I could hear birds calling.

'Look!' said André. Ahead of us two birds were seemingly trying to chase another bird out of a tree. They called sharply: zwee-zwer!

'The two birds with the blue-grey bodies and long orange-brown tail feathers are paradise-flycatchers. The other one with the long crooked beak is a redbilled hornbill.'

After watching the battle for the tree a while longer, we decided to be on our way. A cool breeze picked up, momentarily bringing relief from the scorching sun.

'What are all these brown things?' I had barely said it when I realized it was the dumbest description I could give for the type of plant I had seen growing all around us. It had caught my attention because it was so different from all the others: a dark brown stem protruding from the earth, looking very much like a cigar, but about two or three times longer and thicker. Lengthy green leaves grew out of the top. To me it looked like a kind of miniature palm tree.

'That's a Bushman's candle,' said André. He broke one off, just above the ground. Then he lifted the top part of the plant away. The stem was made of circular bits of fibre, like tightly packed pencil shavings. There was a small indent in the middle. 'The bushmen used to place a hard, glowing coal inside. Then they would put the top back on. The coal would keep on burning. They would carry it around with them until they had to make a fire again.'

'Clever,' I said.

'You can use the leaves as well.' He broke one off and handed it to me. 'Try and break it.'

I tried. It was incredibly strong.

'You could twine a couple together and use it as a rope.'

'Almost like Tarzan's monkey ropes!' I laughed.

'Yeah, almost,' he grinned. 'Come along!'

Walking further, André's keen eyes seemed to survey our surroundings, darting from the ground to the trees, to the sky.

We came across a tawny bird with a black and white breast, wandering around in the underbrush. The bird was about the size of a smallish chicken. 'We call it a swempie in Afrikaans,' said André softly. 'I think it is a coqui francolin in English. Some of them are so tame you could almost touch them. Their call sounds as if they're saying: be-quick, be-quick! The males also have a loud high-pitched crow: kek, KEKekekekekekek.'

The bird turned its head and quickly scampered away. I laughed at André's imitation of the birdcall, loud at first, then gradually becoming softer.

We moved on, stopping regularly so that André could show me things.

'This is a silver cluster-leaf tree.' He picked one of the leaves. It had shiny silver hairs on the upper-side. 'Zulus used the leaves to shine their pots. And if you chew it . . .' He placed it in his mouth and chewed, indicating that I should do the same. I picked a leaf and stuffed it in my mouth, chewing only on the one side. It was almost tasteless. Then I felt it: my mouth went numb on the inside.

André smiled. 'It's good for toothache if there's no dentist around. And speaking of teeth, let me show you this . . .' I followed him further. We stopped at a shrub. 'This is the Kalahari star apple or blue bush.' He cut a stem off with his pocket knife, cleaned the bark off the end and gently started chewing on the exposed yellowish wood. Very soon he was left with a frayed bristled tip. 'This you can use as a toothbrush. You can use the roots as well. At first your mouth will burn and turn yellow, but soon you will have shiny white teeth and fresh breath!'

It was amazing.

André then showed me the weeping wattle, whose leaves could be used as toilet paper. 'Don't confuse it with the common hook-thorn acacia, or what the Zulus call umtholo. The leaves might look the same, but they have little hooked thorns that will ensure a nasty surprise!'

The candelabra tree was a huge succulent tree without any leaves. André scratched the plastic-like green bark with a twig. Within seconds a milky latex seeped through the bark. 'Indigenous people used this fluid to stupefy fish.'

'To help catch them?'

'Yes. By hand.'

I walked around, staring up in amazement at these plants that at first were just clumps of trees to me. Now I saw them in a different light.

André suddenly stopped dead in his tracks, stretching out his hand and touching my shoulder. His eyes were wide with excitement. 'Do you feel it?'

What? I thought. Then . . . the hairs on the back of my neck suddenly stood on end.

Ghoo-oo-oo.

It was like a gust of air. My eyes widened. What the hell was that?

'It's okay. Look, there!' whispered André. He pointed ahead.

What I saw took my breath away.

A gigantic giraffe came strolling by, a mere fifty feet away from us. Its long neck swaying gracefully as it walked. I could hear its hoofs pounding on the ground. Doof, doof, doof!

Its coat shone in the light of the sun. Yellow with dark, almost square marks. Eyes black, long lashes. Horns with tufts of hair on top.

I wanted to step back, but André put me at ease. 'You'll be okay,' he whispered confidently. He certainly wasn't afraid. 'It's a giraffe cow. Her horns are still covered with hair, do you see?' I nodded. 'The bulls' horns are smooth from fighting each other.'

I still remembered the numerous fights I had been in. The cut lips, sore fists. So if I was a giraffe, I thought, my horns would also be smooth by now.

A twig snapped under my feet. The giraffe turned its head, watched us for a while with its black eyes, and then started moving away with steady, graceful strides.

'Beautiful, isn't it?' said André.

I nodded, still completely speechless.

CHAPTER 12

We spent the morning in the bush, and only went back when pangs of hunger overtook us. My legs were tired, feet aching and my skin warm from the sun. I drank the last drop of water from my bottle as we walked down the dust road back to the main building.

Mama Unahti was waiting for us. 'Eh! And what have you two boys been up to?'

'Bush school,' said André grinning.

'I hope you were careful?'

'Don't worry, Mama, Buyi is in good hands.'

She shook her head and clicked her tongue. 'If a lion catches you, don't you come running to me.' We only laughed. She turned, and while making her way back into the building said, 'Come, let me get you some fruit juice. No lunch for you today, the boss is around. He doesn't like it when I feed non-paying customers.'

We followed her past the reception area and the dining room where we'd had breakfast that morning. The TV was playing in the lounge, the volume turned way down. Seeing the familiar flashing images was almost like getting an instant fix. But André dragged me off.

The kitchen was spotless. Mama Unahti poured us each a tall glass from a pitcher. It was the best juice I'd ever had. Sweet and icy cold. Somehow being bone-tired made it taste like heaven.

'We should go swimming now,' said André.

It had been a while since I'd been to a swimming pool. Or at least that's what I hoped he meant – swimming pool, not swimming in a river with crocodiles or something. So I asked him, just to be sure.

'Of course it's in the pool. But we could go to one of the watering holes if you like. And never mind the crocs, you should see the hippos! They kill more people in Africa than any other animal . . .' Again his eyes glimmered mischievously.

It seemed like I had somehow ended up with the most free-spirited person in Africa: a whiteboy with a love for danger.

'No thanks, I think we'll stick to the pool,' I said, hoping that I didn't seem like a girl's blouse.

A Land Rover stopped in front of the building just as we were on our way to get our bathing things. It was our dads, together with a tracker.

'You must be Buyisiwe,' said André's dad. 'I'm Johan.' A tall man. Blonde with a friendly, handsome face.

'Pleased to meet you, sir,' I smiled.

My eyes caught Themba's. 'Hallo,' I said.

He nodded. 'You two been keeping out of trouble, I hope?'

'Yes, Mister Ngonyama,' answered André quickly.

'Stay out of the bush for a while, okay?' he said. It sounded like a command in a way. I instantly knew I shouldn't tell him that we had already been to the bush that very morning.

'Sure,' said André. Then, 'Have you found the lion?'

'No.' My dad's gaze again met mine. 'The footprints were washed away by the rain.'

'He could be anywhere out there. But we'll get him,' said Johan looking back at the rifle in the Land Rover. A shiver ran down my spine when I saw the wooden butt, the black metal barrel. 'Point 375 calibre Remington,' he said smiling.

'Be good, there will be some tourists arriving this afternoon. They're from Japan. Don't bother them, okay?' said Themba. André and I nodded. 'The owner of the resort is also around. Mister Dreyer. Stay out of his way as well. He is not very fond of children.'

André accompanied me to our chalet. We grabbed something to eat. Bread and coffee was all there was. All the other food was frozen. We must have finished the whole loaf of bread, toasting it and eating it with thick spreads of butter and jam.

'Who's this guy?' André asked as we sauntered into my room. He was looking at the poster I had put up the previous night.

'His name is Amir Khan. He is a British boxer, of Pakistani descent. A born fighter is what his dad calls him. He became famous after winning the silver medal in the lightweight division at the 2004 Olympics. And he was only 17! He's since turned professional. Oh yeah, and he actually comes from a long line of warrior kings.'

'So, why do you have him up on your wall?'

'I like boxing, I told you.'

André shrugged, and then turned to me. 'Get your trunks, let's go.'

I didn't have swimming trunks. The nearest I had was a pair of black shorts.

'That will do,' said André. We grabbed a towel from the bathroom and off we went. The pool was near the guest lodges. I marvelled at the stylish buildings and luxury tents scattered around the camp. It seemed very serene here. A few antelope wandered around between the chalets and tents.

'Impala,' said André softly. They stopped what they were doing and turned their heads our way. 'If they hear something they'll instantly try to find out if someone or something has noticed them. If they think you've spotted them, they'll bound off; if not, they'll continue grazing.'

These ones must have seen us watching them. With quick leaps they disappeared.

We had the whole swimming pool to ourselves. It was great fun. Hurtling through the air, diving, splashing, swimming. André tried to duck my head under the water. And I tried to return the favour. Playfully measuring up each other's strength. André was incredibly tough for a boy his age.

Later on we flopped down on our towels, exhausted.

'Your dad said I'd find you here.' I stared up, looking right into the sun. I had to shield my eyes but I recognised the voice. It was Simoshile.

'You should've come earlier,' said André.

'I've only just arrived back from town.'

'How's your dad?'

'You know him. He's ready to take on the world again.'

'Let's go say hi to him,' suggested André, already getting up as if it was a done deal.

I followed suit, knowing what he was after: he wanted to know exactly what had happened the previous night.

We found Lwazi sitting with Mama Unahti at his chalet. She was fussing over him, asking if he was comfortable, offering to send some food over from the kitchen, without the owner, Mister Dreyer, noticing.

'It's terrible,' she cried. 'You poor man!' She threw up her hands and clicked her tongue.

'Oh, look who's come to visit,' said Lwazi, looking relieved to see us.

'How are you doing, Lwazi?' I asked.

'Fine, fine. I just need to keep still for a while. That's what the doctor ordered. Of course, he wanted to keep me there for another day or two, but I refused outright. It is just a scratch. Who stays in hospital for a scratch?' As he said it, his upper body twisted somewhat. He bit back the pain and smiled bravely. 'Besides, they gave me all these pills –'

'Pills?' interrupted Mama 'You haven't said anything to me about pills. Have you started taking them? Don't let me catch you slacking off when it comes to taking medicine. Men never grow up! Always need a woman to look after them.'

Simoshile giggled. Lwazi shrugged helplessly.

'Tell us what happened!' said André, not able to keep his burning curiosity at bay any longer.

Lwazi fell silent for a while, and then he started to recount the night's events. 'The night safari went very well. We saw lots of animals. Even a leopard –'

'A leopard!' shouted André.

'Yes and you know how elusive they are. Excellent camouflage keeps them hidden,' he explained for my benefit.

'But then we ran into trouble. All this rain we've had turns the roads to great pools of mud,' he said, turning to look at me. 'And before long the vehicle got stuck. Johan climbed out to see if there was anything he could do. And then we heard it . . . a lion's roar . . .'

André's eyes suddenly widened. Mine too, I guess.

'It was a deep, terrifying sound, thundering through the dark. I quickly got hold of the search light, and soon found the lion. It was an old one. You could tell by the look of his shabby mane. I tried finding the rest of the pride, but he seemed to be alone.' Lwazi lowered his voice. 'And he was watching us . . . Every move!

'The tourists, of course, were taking photos. Couldn't believe their luck. I don't know what happened, but one of them accidently dropped his camera. The stupid man then got out of the vehicle to pick it up, even though they were warned not to do that. Before we knew it, the lion was heading right for us.

'The tourists screamed. I jumped out of the Land Rover and told them to stay calm. Lions sometimes just want to scare you off, at first charging with all their might, only to stop dead in their tracks a few feet away from you. That is what they teach you in training. But they also teach you that lions become totally different animals at night. It is their hunting time . . .'

Lwazi paused a while, staring each of us in the eye before he continued. 'I had my rifle ready, but I didn't want to use it. I didn't want to kill this beautiful animal just because it had been frightened by a man who didn't do as he was told.

'The lion kept charging. He was now so close that I could see the scar above his left eye. One that he probably got from a fight. The people behind me screamed. Terrified. "Stay calm," I repeated. And then, within seconds it was all over . . .'

'What? Did he kill the man?' asked André breathlessly.

'No,' smiled Lwazi. 'The man had somehow managed to scamper back onto the Land Rover. But I was still there, standing in its way. Staying between the lion and the tourists, like I have been trained. Within seconds the lion was upon me, sinking its teeth right into my shoulder. Here, you see?' he explained, with his hand spread across his shoulder. 'Going for the throat, as they do when hunting. It was then that the shots rang out. It was Johan. The lion fled, disappearing into the night without another sound.'

CHAPTER 13

'Oh goodness!' cried Mama Unahti after hearing the full story. 'Angiphili neze!'

Simoshile chuckled. 'She says she's not feeling well.'

'It is all probably too much for her,' I said, looking at Mama Unahti's distressed face.

'You boys stay out of the bush, you hear me?' cried Mama. 'And to think I took it all very lightly when I heard where you were this morning.'

'You went to the bush?' asked Lwazi and Simoshile simultaneously.

'Please don't tell my dad,' pleaded André.

'It was a stupid thing to do,' said Lwazi shaking his head. 'If you want to go out into the bush, ask your dad to take you along on one of the game drives.'

André and I nodded. Lwazi was right. I knew we shouldn't have gone. But I had already learned so much from just one morning with André, not to mention seeing that splendid giraffe.

Night came all too soon. The end of my first full day in South Africa. I felt tired but somehow happy. I liked André and Simoshile. And Lwazi, and of course Mama Unahti. In just this short while they had made me feel so welcome. It was actually amazing. I had never made friends that quickly. I was always apprehensive when meeting new people. I kept up the walls around me. Fearful of really getting to know them, always wondering if they didn't have a hidden motive for getting to know me.

But with this group of people it was all different. When they talked, they talked from the heart. When they laughed, they did it as if nobody was watching.

Sadly, this was not the case with Themba. The few times I had been in his company I'd felt weirdly disconnected to him. I didn't really know what to say to him. Was it because he hadn't been there for me all those years? I didn't know.

It was around seven in the evening. He still wasn't home. What could he be doing?

I missed having a TV. Probably withdrawal symptoms. I felt fidgety. What was I supposed to do with myself?

Perhaps I should try and cook some sort of meal for Themba. He was sure to be hungry when he got home, all tired. My cooking skills weren't up to much, but I wasn't totally unfamiliar with a kitchen.

There were times back home when Mum didn't want to cook and I simply had to step in if I wanted some dinner.

I grabbed some meat from the fridge and defrosted it in the microwave. It was beef steak. I found some chips as well. Eggs too. Steak, eggs and chips. That will do for a nice dinner!

Busying myself in the kitchen took away the boredom. I thought about the day, and again a smile spread across my face. Wait till I tell Mum about it.

I opened the kitchen door to let some fresh air in. And then I heard it . . . The sound of an animal . . . The lion! The thought flashed through my mind instantly.

No, there was a whine. Do lions whine? I wondered.

Of course not. I listened again, my hand on the doorknob, ready to bang it shut should something leap out at me from the dark. It sounded like a dog.

Should I go out? I was a bit scared, but the animal seemed to be in distress. I found a flashlight in a cupboard. Carefully I made my way outside. Past the tree standing right outside the kitchen. Clenched fist around the torch. The beam of light moved across the ground. And then I saw it: it was a dog, tied up to a tree. A long chain extended right up to its neck. It was an Alsatian. A fine looking animal.

'Hey there, boy!' I said, carefully approaching him. I didn't know if he would bite. He whined again. 'What's your name?' He didn't seem to mind me coming closer. The chain around his neck jingled. He got up, stood there watching me for a while and slowly put one foot in front of the other. Again he whined.

'Hey, there!' I said, softly. I set the light down. He was now right in front of me. I extended my hand slowly. He gave it a quick sniff. He seemed to be okay with me, so I touched him. Scratching him behind the ear. He appeared to like it, and lowered his head. 'Whose dog are you? Themba's?

Why does he keep you all tied up?' The dog turned his head and licked my hand. There was a tag on his collar. Umfana.

'So that's your name, hey, Umfana! I'm Buyisiwe. Buyi for short. I live here now. Why hadn't I seen you earlier? Was it you I heard last night?' Umfana seemed to like the attention. I looked around for his food and water bowls. They were full. So he was well taken care of. It was just this chain that bothered me. My fingers found the clip on the collar. I undid it.

'There you go. Do you want to join me in the house?' I picked up the flashlight again. The dog stayed back, sitting on his haunches. Looking at me. 'Come, boy!'

He got up slowly, his head lowered but his eyes looking up at me.

'Come!'

He followed me into the house, warily. Looking around.

Suddenly I caught the smell of something burning. The food! I'd forgotten all about it. I raced to the stove and turned down the heat. What a miserable sight! The steak had only just stopped short of being embers. The chips were, to say the least, extremely crispy. Luckily I hadn't started on the eggs.

Umfana stared up at me. He tilted his head to the side. His black eyes were seemingly sorry for the mess I had made.

'So much for dinner then,' I said trying to scrape some of the black bits off the steak. 'Jamie Oliver would be pleased to know that I'm not in competition with him.'

I put on a CD and went to my room. Umfana followed me. I opened the window. The sounds of night came flowing in with the evening breeze. Bloc Party on the right, Africa on the left.

'Now there's a combination for you, hey Umfana?' I said pulling my fingers through his coat.

Themba came home around nine. I got up from my bed.

'Hallo,' I said. 'How was your day?' The words sounded stupid. Contrived like a third-rate sitcom. But I had to start making an effort to get to know this man.

'Fine,' he said and sighed. His clothes were all wrinkled and dusty.

'I made some dinner. Or at least I tried. I haven't eaten yet. I decided to wait till you got home.'

'What did you make? Smells like something burned . . .'

'Steak and chips. I just need to warm it up again. And fry up some eggs.'

'You cook then?'

'Well, I'm no Jamie Oliver, but –'

'Jamie who?'

'This English guy . . . The naked chef.'

Themba frowned. I suddenly realised how it must have sounded to him. Naked chef!

'Never mind,' I said.

'Is this it?' he asked pointing to the steamed up glass bowl. He removed the lid. 'You did burn it. Meat is expensive! And this . . . this is a waste.' His cold stare was fixed on me.

I felt my insides churning. I'd just tried to do some good.

'Anyway, I had dinner with the guests,' he continued. 'I mostly do, remember that. It's part of my job. Answering their questions, mingling, making sure they get what they're paying for: the best African experience possible.' He sighed. 'I only eat at home on my off-days.'

Themba's voice was almost void of emotion. He is just tired, I said to myself.

And Themba was probably right. It was a waste of good food. But something inside me wanted some recognition for at least trying.

I followed him out of the kitchen as he made his way to his room. When he stepped back out again moments later, he had his shirt off. His bare chest and arms rippled with muscles. Like that of a boxer, I thought.

My dad looked like a boxer.

On his way to the bathroom, Themba suddenly stopped. He had noticed something. 'What's that dog doing in the house?' he asked firmly.

Umfana was lying stretched out in front of the couch. He whined and lowered his head.

'Get him out! Dogs don't belong inside!' Themba's voice boomed. I shrunk back against the wall. 'And tie him up before he goes off killing animals.'

CHAPTER 14

Morning broke. I was in a bad mood. What the hell was I doing here at all? Themba obviously didn't like me. I wasn't the son he wanted. Perhaps too much of a poncey English boy for his taste. But what did he expect?

Mum also hadn't called the previous night like I had expected. I hoped she was all right.

André and Simoshile came knocking later in the day. My mood lifted.

'I'm so bored,' sighed André.

'You'll just have to get used to it,' said Simoshile.

'Ek wens hulle wil nou daardie blerrie leeu vang en klaarkry!'

I frowned. What was that? Simoshile translated. 'He says he wishes they would just catch that bloo . . . um, that lion and be done with it.'

'We can at least move around in the main camp. That would be okay, wouldn't it?' I tried. 'It isn't as if we should stay inside all day.'

'Buyi is right,' said Simoshile. 'Let's go for a swim.'

'Yeah!' I shouted.

André moaned, saying something about it not being the same. That he wanted to go to the bush. Nonetheless he followed us to the pool.

All our troubles were soon forgotten once we dived into the crystal clear water. The coolness enveloping us.

A flurry of voices caught our attention. It was the Japanese visitors. They were huddled together near one of the guest chalets.

'They've just returned from their morning walk with one of the rangers,' said Simoshile. 'That's probably what's got them all excited.'

'Why can they go to the bush, but we can't?' I asked.

Simoshile rolled her eyes. 'Because the ranger carries a rifle!'

'Oh yeah, right. I forgot.'

'Something's really got them going, look,' said André, stretching his neck to see what it was.

They were all chatty. Laughing, while trying to arrange themselves into a group. One of them tried to get a photo of the others. But something was amiss.

'It's the tortoise,' said Simoshile.

'The what?' I said.

'There, on the grass. It's a tortoise. They're all trying to have their picture taken with it.'

Now I saw it. The tortoise didn't seem interested in his fifteen minutes of fame. As soon as the Japanese tourists had organised themselves into a group, all smiling for the camera, the tortoise had moved along. And they had to re-organise themselves all over again a few feet further on.

They seemed to be enjoying it though, bursting out in fits of laughter every now and again. And when they finally got it right, they switched photographers and the madness started all over again.

I sat watching them with a gaping mouth. Every now and again I could hear André and Simoshile chuckling.

Then, all satisfied, they disappeared to their chalets and tents. The tortoise was finally left to make its way back to the bush in peace.

Mama Unahti sensed our frustration when we aimlessly hung around the main building after returning from the pool.

'Oh my children, my children,' she said, her body jiggling as she slapped her hands together. 'What's wrong?'

'We're bored,' said André.

Her face lit up. 'Nonsense! There's plenty to do.'

'But we want to go to the bush.'

'No, you heard what Lwazi said. Do you want to become that scarred lion's prey?'

'But –'

'No buts. There's a lot to do. Just look around you.'

'Like what?' asked André.

'Go climb a tree,' she answered.

'Girls don't climb trees,' said Simoshile screwing up her face.

Mama Unahti clicked her tongue. 'Ah! Says who? Go, go, go! Before Mister Dreyer sees you.'

I don't think Mum would believe me if I told her, but I climbed a tree that day. Simoshile stayed behind on the ground. 'I'll keep a lookout for snakes,' was her excuse.

'Yeah, right,' scoffed André as he made his way up. 'As if you would be able to see a boomslang from down there.'

Could there really be snakes up there, I wondered. A shiver ran down my spine. I decided to keep my eyes peeled and didn't really bother with the amazing view from the tree.

The day dragged on. We went back to my home, deciding to play with Umfana. He enjoyed all the attention. And being able to run around freely for a while.

It broke my heart to tie him up again when André and Simoshile left.

I sat alone in the chalet, my thoughts were my only company. Waiting for the phone to ring. Wondering if I should call Mum. Better not, I thought. Not before I have permission from Themba.

The next three days were all much the same, dragging along endlessly. Until at last André called. 'I've had enough of this! Let's go to the watering hole. Who wants to foefieslide?'

CHAPTER 15

'Foefie, what?'

'Foefieslide!' cried André. 'Don't you know what that is?'

'No,' I answered hesitantly. Was I supposed to know?

André's eyes again had that mischievous gleam. Apparently Simoshile knew, but the look on André's face begged her: don't tell him yet.

'And what about the lion?' asked Simoshile.

'What about the lion?' shrugged André. 'He probably ran off to one of the other game reserves after that shot that was fired. Don't you think they would have found him by now if he was still around?'

'Probably. But I'm still scared to go.'

'Oh come on, Simoshile! You and I have been to the watering hole a hundred times. Why are you scared now?'

'Because my dad warned us.'

'And so he should have. That's his job, remember. He's your dad! But we're not children anymore. We can look after ourselves.'

'Not in the bush,' said Simoshile. 'Things can happen and you know it. Bad things . . .' There was dread behind Simoshile's words.

I listened to the two of them reasoning it out. And I agreed with both of them. On the one hand I was bored out of my skull sitting around doing nothing. But on the other hand there was the fear of the lion and goodness knows what other animals.

'Look,' said André finally, 'even Buyi is keen on going.'

Where did he get that from, I wondered. I hadn't said a word.

'Okay,' said Simoshile, 'I'll only go if Buyi goes.'

Their eyes turned to me. Now I have to make the decision? My mind raced on furiously. Why me? Did Simoshile trust me that much? Or was there more to it?

'Come on, Englishman!' André egged me on.

I couldn't stand it any longer. Before I knew, I nodded sheepishly.

André's smile almost ran right round his face. 'Good! Let's go!'

We were in the Namhlanje camp. Water bottles in hand, sunscreen on our faces, and towels over our shoulders. We tried to look brave, but I could see even André looked a bit tense. He surveyed our surroundings with his keen eyes. I tried to as well, but my eyes weren't as sharp as his.

We came across some zebras and stopped to watch them for a while.

'Is a zebra white with black stripes, or black with white stripes?' asked Simoshile softly.

'I don't know.'

She only giggled, and never gave me the answer. I didn't mind though. I simply treasured the moment of seeing my first real-life zebra ever.

'You would usually find zebra grazing with blue wildebeest,' whispered André. 'The wildebeest depend on the zebra's superior vision and hearing in case of a predator attack.'

'And the zebras tolerate the wildebeest because if they do get attacked, the predators would most probably go for the slower wildebeest,' added Simoshile.

As with most animals they didn't like to be stared at, not knowing what our intentions were. They moved on, disappearing into the bush.

I told Simoshile about the trees André had shown me the other day. She seemed to hang on every word I said. Listening so intently that for a moment I almost thought . . . No, it couldn't be. It was all my imagination.

'Did he show you the marula tree?' she asked after a while.

'No, not yet.'

'You have to, André,' she said. 'It is my favourite. It has this delicious tasting fruit. About the size of plums. Animals love it too. Monkeys, kudu, duiker, impala. Even the elephants. You can make jelly, jam and even beer from the fruit.'

'But,' interrupted André, 'there's something else she's dying to tell you about this tree.'

Simoshile gave André a shove. 'Go play with the lions!'

André laughed. 'Go ahead and tell him, Simoshile!'

'No, I'm not going to. Not now.' She suddenly appeared shy.

'Then I shall.'

'Do it then.'

'What is it?' I asked.

André playfully placed his hands under his chin, fluttered his eyes and said in a girlish voice, 'The Zulu people call the marula tree the marriage tree. Isn't that sweet?'

'You're just being silly now,' said Simoshile turning her head away.

'The marriage tree? Why?' I asked.

'The tree symbolizes fertility –'

'André! Stop!' cried Simoshile.

' – tenderness and early maturity . . .'

I almost choked. So that's why Simoshile didn't want to continue with her story.

André seemed to enjoy angering Simoshile. 'They use a brew of the bark in a cleansing ritual before marriage.'

'I'm not talking to you anymore,' snapped Simoshile.

'Yes, you are!'

'No, I'm not. I should never have come along with you. You're such a . . . such a . . .'

'. . . handsome bloke!' cried André. 'Oh, no, sorry. I forgot we're talking about me now, and not Buyi!'

I almost bit my tongue. What was this? Did Simoshile think I'm handsome?

She walked on ahead, arms crossed over her chest.

'Now you did it,' I whispered to André. Then: 'Did she really say I'm handsome?'

He nodded. 'You'd better hope we don't come across any marula trees on the way, Buyi, or you might just find yourself a married man before the sun sets today!'

If I weren't black, I would have blushed.

After an hour's walk we finally reached the watering hole. It was about half the size of a soccer field. And seemingly a deep dam of water. There was a high embankment on one side with lots of trees. The other side was cleared of all trees and plants. The sun reflected sharply on the yellow sand.

'This is just one of the watering holes in the resort. Animals usually gather here in the afternoon. See, there's a look-out point.' André indicated a wooden structure very much like a tower. It had an enclosed platform on top where you could sit and watch the animals. There were, however, no animals in sight now, only some wild ducks and other water birds.

'Are you still wondering about that foefieslide?' he asked. 'Let me show you.' Simoshile trailed behind us now. I think she had lost all interest in this adventurous expedition of ours.

I followed André to a tall tree, planted firmly on the raised embankment.

'There . . .' he said, pointing up at the branches. I saw a cable tied to a thick branch and running all the way across the watering hole to the other side. A pulley attached to a handle bar was fixed to the cable.

'A zip line!' I said. 'That's what we call it.'

'Great isn't it? Ever been on one?'

'No never. I've only seen it on TV. Is it safe?'

'Of course. You want to try it?'

We steadily made our way up the tree. I was getting good at this. Before long we were up there amongst the branches, looking down at the ground. It hadn't even crossed my mind that there might be snakes in the tree.

'Do you want to go first?' André asked.

'Um . . . I think you'd better go,' I said hesitantly. 'I'll watch.'

'Okay then.' André gripped the handle bar firmly. He inhaled deeply.

'Wait!' I cried. 'Aren't you going to put on a helmet or something? Or a safety strap?'

'No.'

'It's a long drop, isn't it? What if you fall?'

'Then you kind of crash into the water and hope the crocodiles have eaten already.'

'What? Are there crocodiles in the water?'

'No, Buyi, I'm just messing with you. Relax.'

Easy for you to say, I thought.

'Ready? Here I go-o-o!'

I watched André soar across the water, hanging on by only his hands. His body flying out behind him.

'Yo-hee-ee!' he cried.

Reaching the other side, he swung his legs forward, his feet touching the water momentarily, and then the sand. He ran the last few paces, stopping just short of the anchor pole.

My heart started racing as I watched André unclipping the pulley. He made his way around the watering hole, running past Simoshile, who was sitting on the embankment and twining together lengths of grass.

She ignored him totally.

André climbed back up the tree. I felt the tension rising in me.

'There you go!' said André, handing me the pulley bar. He showed me how to fix it to the cable, and patted me on the back. 'All yours, Englishman!'

This was the moment. I breathed deeply. I tried not to look down. My hands were already sweaty. I wiped them on the back of my trousers.

Small bubbles appeared on the surface of the water. I barely noticed. My eyes were fixed on the cable. Measuring the distance. Don't be a such a coward, I told myself.

Then!

I leaped from the tree. Instantly my weight bore down on my hands, my fingers. The wind rushed past my face, my body flying back.

It was great! Just like soaring through the sky . . . I could breathe again.

Then it happened! A sudden cry: 'Watch out! Hippos!'

My moment of euphoria was gone in an instant. The small bubbles I had seen earlier grew bigger. Waves appeared. Then a head almost the size of a kitchen table. Dark brown.

They kill more people in Africa than any other animal, André's words returned to me.

I was caught up in an instant panic. My hands sweating. How far still? Far enough.

Damn that André! Why hadn't he told me there were hippos? And that joke he made about the crocodiles . . . For all I knew he was lying about that too!

I felt my hands slipping.

Another hippo appeared, gazing up at me. It opened its mouth. Never before had the colour pink seem so threatening. The bulky teeth. White and strong.

I'm not going to make it. The embankment was still too far off. It seemed like the ride would never end. Why was André's over so fast? Oh yeah, there weren't any hippos waiting to swallow him down in one gulp.

'Hang on,' I said to myself, trying to muster up some courage. 'You can do this. Just hang on.'

I heard the splashing hippos. Gloump!

One of them disappeared momentarily. It reappeared within a heartbeat.

'Buyisiwe!' Simoshile cried out again.

André's voice too came rolling across the water. 'Just stay calm. It will be all right. They're just nosy. They won't hurt you.'

The other side of the embankment was only a few feet away now. My feet nearing the surface of the water as the cable slanted downwards. I raised my knees up to my chest, trying to keep my feet dry. Out of reach of any hippos or crocs or other man-eating animals.

Nearly there, nearly there . . .

Soft sand below my feet. At last! I've never been so pleased to touch ground. I ran the last few steps on the sand but still holding on to the pulley car, like André had. In those last moments my hands slipped and I fell forward, sending up a spray of sand.

Instantly I scrambled back to my feet. Hippos are land animals too. And they are fast as lightning. I didn't look back. The lookout point was close by. I kept my eyes fixed on it. Praying that I would reach it before any hippo caught up with me.

Grass rustled behind me.

No!

Don't look back!

Run!

My legs felt weak, but somehow I found the strength to carry me further.

I reached the lookout tower not a minute too soon. I knew for certain there was something behind me. I could see it from the corner of my eye.

I grabbed the ladder. A splinter tore into my hand, but I didn't care. I hurried up the rungs. Breathlessly.

The thing was still behind me. Could hippos climb ladders?

I felt it touch my ankle. Kicked back.

Laughter.

Silly laughter. It was André. 'Jeez, Englishman. I didn't think you had it in you. Sprinting like that. If I didn't know any better I would have sworn there was a wild animal on your tail!'

CHAPTER 16

'Stop laughing, would you!' I said as we made our way back home. André and Simoshile burst out in fits of laughter every now and again, the feud between the two of them forgotten.

'Sorry, Buyi, I can't help it,' said Simoshile, clutching her stomach.

'You should have seen yourself,' said André.

'Arms and legs flailing,' cried Simoshile.

'You looked like one of those people in horror movies. Wha-a-a-a!' André gave his impression of my hippo getaway. 'Wha-a-a-a!'

'I didn't scream,' I said, trying to defend myself.

'Yes you did!' they cried with laughter.

'Well, I don't think so. Anyway, I was scared, okay? You would have been too.'

'Those hippos were probably just amazed when they saw a flying Englishman above their watering hole. That's why they didn't make a move.'

'One of them actually opened its mouth just as I was passing overhead,' I said. Why couldn't they see the danger I was in?

'The hippo was probably laughing too,' said André. 'I can just imagine what the view from the bottom must have been like if the view from the side was so funny!'

'If you knew about the hippos, why did you let me foef . . . whatever over them?'

Simoshile answered, 'It isn't their usual spot. They prefer another watering hole a distance away. I was actually surprised to see them there.'

'And that's why you screamed?'

'I had to warn you.'

'There you are then! You knew I was in danger. And you too, André. Or else you wouldn't have come sprinting round the watering hole. You knew I might be in trouble!'

'I came running to make sure you . . .'

'I what?' I challenged.

'You know . . . that you didn't fall on your butt trying to get off the foefieslide.'

'That lie far exceeds the size of a hippo's opened jaws,' I smiled. André had a silly grin on his face. He shook his head. They both knew I'd been in quite a bit of danger, but making light of it somehow eased the tension.

And now forever more I would be the butt of all hippo jokes.

'Wha-a-a-a!' cried André again, running up the road like a madman. I caught Simoshile's eye. She smiled at me. Something inside me felt strange, so I quickly looked away.

André had meanwhile stopped his charade. He stood there in the middle of the dusty road. His head tilted to the side. 'Shush!' he whispered.

We all listened. Suddenly they both looked around wildly. André's face turned pale.

Oemfff . . . Oemfff . . .

'Lion!' whispered Simoshile.

'Is it him?' I whispered back. 'The one who . . .'

'Don't know,' said André, his eyes wide. 'But I don't think I want to find out . . . Run!'

It was like a gunshot had gone off indicating the start of a race. A race to live. The dust billowed in fear-filled yellow clouds beneath our feet. The road stretched out ahead of us.

Oemfff . . . Oemfff . . .

'Where is it?' I panted.

'Don't know. Just keep going,' whispered André.

I couldn't even determine the direction of the sound. The lion could have been anywhere. That scared me.

Were André and Simoshile playing a trick on me again? I had never heard a lion roar before that day. In fact, the closest

I'd ever come to a lion was the statues in Trafalgar Square.

I could hear my own breath coming hard, burning in my chest. André and Simoshile were heaving too. This was no joke. For the second time in one day I was running away from a wild animal. Scared out of my wits.

I don't know how far we ran, or for how long, before André eventually said, 'Come on you guys, not much . . . further now.' His voice almost disappeared under his breath. He turned his head again. Listening. I did too. I couldn't hear the lion anymore. That didn't mean it wasn't there.

Up ahead we saw the Namhlanje gate.

'I can't run anymore,' moaned Simoshile, holding her side and clenching her teeth.

'Just a few steps more,' encouraged André.

I felt just like Simoshile. I hadn't had much exercise in years. And now it was taking its toll. I had a pain in my side. My mouth was dry, my legs weak.

André ran up ahead, opening the gate for us.

As we crashed through it, relief washed over us. I heard the gate slam shut. We were safe.

Just then we heard the drone of an engine. Rangers!

'Hurry, or we'll get into trouble!' cried André. We scrambled off to a clump of trees beside the road, dropped down to the ground and waited . . . breathlessly.

CHAPTER 17

The Land Rover drove past. Inside were Themba and Lwazi.

Lwazi had a rifle with him. The Land Rover stopped at the Namhlanje gate. Lwazi got out to open it. He stopped for a moment, looking around as if he had heard something.

No, please! I begged silently.

Time seemed to stretch on endlessly.

'What's wrong?' asked Themba.

Lwazi shrugged and lifted the latch off the gate. Themba made his way through. We watched in stunned silence as Lwazi closed the gate again.

That was really close.

A thunderstorm broke out that afternoon. Flashes of lightning shattering the darkened sky.

I stood at the front door, gazing at the spectacle, but shrinking back every time a bolt of lightning came thundering down, echoing against the Waterberg.

Suddenly I heard a fear-filled yelping.

'Umfana!' The word was almost like a cry. 'I'm coming!'

The rain came pouring down now. Huge drops knocking holes in the dry sand. I guess I should have taken an umbrella, but it was too late to turn back now. I was already soaked.

Umfana strained at his chain. His tail wagging anxiously.

'Don't worry,' I said. But it didn't calm him down. The yelps were louder now. His body twisting and turning, making it difficult for me to undo the catch on his collar.

Another crash of lightning.

It was quite close.

'Got it!' I sighed as the clip opened. 'Come, boy!'

We were both soaked to the bone as we stepped into the chalet. But at least we were out of the storm. I fetched a towel from the bathroom, and undressed, leaving my wet clothes in a heap on the floor. I dried myself before slipping on another pair of jeans.

Umfana had already started shaking his coat dry in the kitchen. 'No!' I cried. 'Do you want the old man to freak out?' I used my towel to dry him properly. He still smelled like a wet dog. My towel too. I dropped it on the heap of wet clothes in my room.

The rain came down hard now, splodging the windows. Umfana kept on whining every time the thunder boomed.

'Would you like me to put on some music?' I asked. 'It will drown out the thunder. Do you like British bands? Or do you prefer American? Sorry, I don't have any African music.'

Umfana tilted his head, listening intently. As if he understood every word I said. I loved it!

'British it is then!'

Soon the sounds of Razorlight filled the chalet. I almost didn't hear the telephone ringing. Turning down the volume on the hi-fi, I answered the phone.

'Hey, Buyi!'

'Mum!'

'Are you doing well?'

'You know me.'

'Making friends?'

I told her about André and Simoshile. Leaving out the bit about the marriage tree.

'And how is Africa?'

'Way different from London. And guess what, it's raining here!'

'Oh bother! Can't get away from the rain, can you?'

'At least it doesn't rain for days on end here. Most days are sunny and extremely hot.'

'Are you and your dad coping?'

'Yeah,' I lied, 'we get along fine. Don't worry.'

'You should help out around the house. Don't sit around watching TV all day, you hear me?'

'TV? He doesn't even have one!'

'No television? That must be doing you a load of good. And the fresh air too.'

'No scarcity of that in the bush!'

We talked and laughed for quite a while. I kept quiet about my encounter with the hippos and the lion. It would just upset Mum. She complained about work, the neighbours who'd had a huge fight, soccer hooligans taking to the streets after last night's game.

And eventually we had to say goodbye.

I sat there with a stupid grin on my face, thankful to have heard Mum's voice again. Glad that she was coping.

Umfana fell asleep with his head on my lap. I let my fingers run through his coat and watched his ears twitch every now and again.

The thunder had stopped but it was still raining, the mellow scent of soaked plants and sodden earth rushing into the chalet. Inhaling it deeply, I leaned back on the couch. For the first time in quite a while I felt happy.

I must have dozed off, but was woken an hour later by the sound of a Land Rover's engine.

Themba!

I was on my feet in a flash. Umfana was still in the house. 'Come boy!' I whispered. 'Come!' He wasn't too keen on going back out into the rain. I opened the kitchen door and pushed him out. Just in time.

The front door opened. I heard Themba stamping his feet at the door, probably to get some of the mud off his shoes.

'Hi, Themba.'

I saw him taking off his shoes and socks before he entered. His clothes were soaked like mine had been earlier. Perhaps even worse. His legs and chest were splattered with mud.

'We got caught in the rain,' he said, taking off his shirt. He wiped the rain off his forehead. 'Have you had dinner?'

I shook my head. Now that he mentioned it, I did feel hungry.

'Why not?' he asked.

'I fell asleep on the couch.'

'You should eat when I'm not here. There's food in the cupboard and the fridge. I can't hang around preparing breakfast, dinner and lunch for you, Buyisiwe. I've got to work. And I don't want you carrying stories to Mama Unahti about me not taking care of you.'

'I never said that.'

'That's what she told me. I don't have time to babysit you, Buyi. You understand?'

I nodded.

'What is this mess?' he asked, pointing to the heap of wet clothes and the towel.

'I was also caught in the rain.'

'Clean it up!'

I scrambled to pick it up. He watched me all the while.

'What should I do with it?'

'Wash it.'

What? Luckily I didn't say it. His eyes rested sternly on me. I'd never done my own washing. Mum always took care of it. There was a heap of dirty clothes in my room as well. For the past few days I'd watched the heap grow, wondering who would do it.

'There's a washing machine under the counter in the kitchen. After you've finished, hang the clothes inside the chalet. They'll be dry in the morning. Tomorrow you can do the rest of your washing as well. The rain will probably clear up tonight. You can hang those clothes outside. There is a washing line.'

'How does the machine work?'

'Figure it out.'

I stood frozen to the spot. Figure it out?

'What are you waiting for Buyi?'

'Nothing.'

'Then get a move on.'

He disappeared into his room. I stuffed my wet clothes into the washer and as I frowned down at the dials at the front, I heard Themba's voice again. Right beside me.

'You haven't been going out into the camps, have you?'

I gulped. 'No, sir . . . no.'

Did he know I was lying? His face was emotionless. 'We saw that lion again today. The one with the scar. He was in the Namhlanje camp.'

'Oh,' was all I managed to get out as my heart started racing.

'He got away from us again.'

'But at least you know which camp he is in.'

'For now. They can move up to 20 km per day. He might be somewhere else tomorrow.'

'But the fences would stop him, wouldn't they?'

'They didn't stop him before. Lwazi was attacked in the Izolo camp. The fences linking the camps aren't up to scratch anymore, thanks to the elephants. For now we just make sure the fences round the main camp are kept in good condition. To keep the visitors safe.' Themba fell silent before he added, 'Apparently this lion was seen at a small settlement a distance away.'

'How do you know it was him?'

'He had the same scar above his left eye.' Themba sighed heavily, his strong shoulders drooping suddenly. 'The people said he killed a man. If this is true, he has turned man-eater. We'll have to get rid of him as soon as possible.'

'Get rid of him? Catch him, you mean?'

'We'll have to shoot him, Buyi. But he is clever. He has already eluded us twice. Not even Lwazi could pick up his track. And he's one of our best trackers. This scarred lion doesn't seem to mind moving about in the rain. That's unusual for a lion. But then again, in the game of survival nothing is unusual.'

CHAPTER 18

André and Simoshile were already waiting for me at the main building.

'Sanibona!' I said, greeting them and showing off what little I knew of isiZulu.

'Sawubona. Unjani?' said Simoshile.

'I'm doing well. What do we have planned for the day?'

André sighed. 'Nothing.'

'I've already told André I'm not falling for his sweet talk again today,' said Simoshile.

'Yeah, yeah,' moaned André.

'I'm not going to go off wandering around in any of the camps. Not even Kusasa.'

'It's probably a good thing,' I said and told them about the lion who had killed somebody in a nearby village.

'There, you see, André?' said Simoshile. 'All the more reason for us to stay right here where we are safe.'

'You guys don't have an adventurous bone in your bodies,' he grumbled, his face gloomy. But then it suddenly lit up.

'Oh no!' said Simoshile. 'I know that look. He's got a plan again.'

'You're right, sister! Wait here!'

He jumped up and disappeared into the building. Moments later he returned with Mama Unahti. I smiled as I saw her beautifully coloured dress, her kind face.

She gave me a quick hug. 'André tells me you want to go on a game drive?'

André's eyes widened, indicating to us to just go along with it.

'Uh, yeah,' I stammered.

'Mmm . . . I'll see what I can do. Themba and Lwazi are taking some guests out on a game drive this morning. Just three of them. There will be place for three more.'

A game drive! That would be so cool!

André smiled, satisfied.

'Wait here, I'll radio them to see if it is all right.'

We waited for half an hour, and in the mean time enjoyed some strong coffee and something André called 'beskuit'. It was pieces of baked and oven dried dough, dotted with aniseeds. He dunked his in the coffee and ate with great gusto. It seemed a bit strange to me, but when I tried it I found it quite tasty. Slightly sweet with a liquorice aftertaste, but good.

When the tourists arrived, we tried to keep out of their way. We didn't want to bother them, but eventually they started chatting to us, so we just went along with it.

'My name is Moira,' said the woman. 'This is my husband Frank.'

'And I'm Tom. A family friend,' said the third one.

'We're from Chicago. United States of America, you know.'

But we could easily have guessed they were from America. Their loud voices and heavy accents gave them away.

André stole the show, telling them about all his exploits in the bush. I wondered if half of them weren't just made up on the spot to impress the visitors. They seemed to enjoy it, laughing at his jokes and oo-ing and ah-ing at regular intervals. Moira wondered aloud if she had brought along enough medicine in case 'a wild beast goes rampant'. She ruffled through her bag, eventually standing there with what seemed like a small pharmacy in her hand.

'Oh, put that away, Moira,' hissed her husband.

The Land Rover arrived.

'Good morning, good morning!' said Themba. He introduced Lwazi and himself to the group. He seemed to be in a very good mood. Lwazi also greeted everybody, winking at us. He seemed to have recovered well after the lion attack. I was sure Mama Unahti had taken really good care of him these past couple of days.

'Before we take you into the bush, there are a couple of things you need to be aware of. Please, it is for your own safety.' Themba went through a whole list of dos and don'ts, his face stern, and his voice urgent but caring. 'Your safety lies not only in my hands, but also in your own.'

He finished his short speech with a hearty, 'Off we go then!' I noticed he didn't mention anything about the man-eating lion wandering about.

'You guys behave, all right?' Themba whispered to me as we got into the open Land Rover. I nodded. André, Simoshile and I got into the back, with the visitors taking the seats in front of us. Themba was at the steering wheel and Lwazi sat perched on the tracker's seat on the bonnet.

'Buyi, do you want to sit next to Simoshile?' asked André with a playful glint in his eye.

'No. Why?' I asked.

'I'm just asking,' he sniggered. Simoshile elbowed him in the ribs and rolled her eyes.

I saw the rifle gleaming in the front of the Land Rover. We would be safe, I said to myself as the thought of a man-eating lion crossed my mind again.

Lwazi opened the Izolo camp gate. Themba drove through, waited for Lwazi to catch up and then started up the dusty road. He told us all about the quartzite that is found in the area. Quartzite, he explained, is a type of rock formed by pressurised and heated sandstone. The iron oxide inside it gives it a distinctive white to pink appearance.

Themba moved on to the history of the area, elaborating on tin mining in the Waterberg Mountains. Apparently there were still open mining holes in the mountain, where bats lived and animals sometimes hid.

'What's that?' asked Tom, pointing to a strange looking device planted in a clearing. There was a small can at the top and something that looked like a trough at the bottom. They were connected by a ribbed pole.

Themba explained: 'That's what we call a salt lick. The tray at the bottom is filled with thermo-phosphate, salt, maize meal and bone meal. It provides proteins and minerals for the animals.'

'Oh, almost like taking your daily vitamins!' said Moira.

'Yes, almost,' grinned Themba. 'The strange contraption has another use as well. The animals in the bush are pestered by ticks. It would be impossible to catch and dip them all like cattle. So that little can on top contains some oil mixed with dip. It slowly trickles down that ribbed surface. And while the animals' heads are down in the feeding tray, their necks and ears gets covered with the dip.'

'Oh very clever!' said Moira.

'Did you know that?' I asked André.

'Of course!' he replied.

The sun fell golden across the sandy road we were travelling on. There were tracks everywhere. I noticed Lwazi keeping his eyes fixed on these tracks. At one section of the road the leaves of the trees formed a roof overhead, bringing momentary relief from sun.

We came across a herd of impala. Themba switched off the engine. We watched in silence, and then Themba explained how these antelope have special glands, located at a tuft of black hair on the lower legs. 'When attacked they secrete pheromones from these glands. The pungent smell lingers in the air, throwing their attackers off track. The herd re-group again later by following this scent.'

'Impala tracks look like a primitive spear point,' said Lwazi, turning back in his seat, 'the tip ending in a particularly deep tread.'

With a smile Themba added. 'We also jokingly refer to these antelope as McDonald's.'

'Why?' asked Moira.

Themba must have been waiting for that question: 'Do you see the singular black lines on either side of their behinds, and the one on their tails? It forms a MacDonald's M.'

The tourists laughed heartily. I did too.

'Those black lines,' whispered André, leaning over to my side, 'attract more heat than the white surrounding area. Ticks just love the warmth, so they gather there, and keep away from the impala's arse and ... you know what ...'

'I heard that André,' called Themba from the front of the Land Rover.

'Sorry sir!'

'Is it true?' asked Frank.

'Indeed it is,' said Themba.

Driving off again we marvelled as the scenery changed with every bend in the road. Then Lwazi raised his hand. Themba stopped.

'Come look at this,' said Lwazi, bending down. We got out of the Land Rover. 'You can read the story of the bush in the tracks left behind in the sand. Do you see here?' He pointed to one of the tracks. 'This is a blue wildebeest spoor. The hind leg. See how it almost forms a triangle with the top chopped off?'

Lwazi moved on a bit, now pointing at another set of tracks. 'This belongs to a jackal. It is shaped like a Christmas tree. And that one there . . . is a serval's tracks.'

'How do you know if the tracks are fresh?' asked Tom.

'Well, it rained last night and you can see these tracks were made into the mud. But if it hasn't been raining you can look at the edges of the track. Have they already started crumbling in? Then it is an old track. Or in the early morning you can be on the lookout for dew inside the tracks. If there is dew in the surrounding area, but not inside the track, you know it is fresh.'

We got back into the Land Rover. Moving on we stopped to look at some waterbuck, with the distinctive white ring on their black behinds. Themba called it a toilet ring because it looked just like one was stuck to the animal. We also saw some kudu. 'The ghosts of the bush,' Themba called them, 'because they are hard to find and can disappear almost in an instant.'

'Oh look!' cried Moira, pointing to an almost black haze darting across the road ahead, right through a fence, and scampering off. I think there were about four of them. One large animal and three smaller ones. Their tales pointing up like little antennas.

'Warthogs!' said Themba.

'Oh they look so sweet – the little ones!' cooed Moira. 'How did they get through the fence so quickly?'

Themba drove up to the fence showing us the old, used, motor car tyres placed at regular intervals at the foot of the fence. 'They are just big enough for the warthogs to scamper through on their knees. We sometimes find that poachers set up traps here. Or they set them in the footpaths that animals like to use.'

'Traps?' cried Moira.

'What kind of traps?' asked Frank.

'They are usually very simple: just a long piece of wire, tied around and slipped through an eye, forming a noose. The poachers don't care if they hurt the animals. And if they catch something that they don't want, they just leave it there to die.'

'Terrible!' shrieked Moira.

We drove on and after a while reached a place called Picnic Rock. Large, yellow-brown boulders were stacked on top of each other, covered here and there by trees, shrubs and smaller underbrush.

Themba stopped and switched off the engine. 'If you would follow me,' he said like a true gentleman. 'Mama Unahti has packed us a basket of fruit and confectionaries. We can enjoy it while taking in the splendid view from the top of the hill. But be careful, this is a favourite spot for leopards. They just love lying here, basking in the sun.'

Moira giggled nervously. She probably thought it was a joke.

'Do you think she would be able to outrun a leopard if one came charging down the hill?' I whispered to André.

'No ways, she'll be the first one he catches. At least we only need to outrun her if something happens. It's like the relationship between the zebras and blue wildebeest that I told you about! Blue wildebeest are easy prey because of the zebra's agility.'

I sniggered. Simoshile seemed to think we were very rude.

We made our way up the boulders, Moira heaving heavily. At least there was someone around in worse shape than me.

There were no leopards on Picnic Rock. I breathed a silent sigh of relief. Themba was right; the view from up there was incredible. He showed us where the boundaries of the resort ran. It was an enormous place. I'd never before seen so many shades of green. There were clearings intermingled with areas that looked like lumps of green clay stuck together. And everything was drenched in terrific sunlight.

Up there we could hear birds calling clearly, also the continuous buzz of cicadas. Sounds rushing in from all directions. The light breeze cooling our hot bodies. Fresh air filling our lungs.

Even the food tasted great.

'There,' said Simoshile, pointing to a clump of trees. 'Giraffes.'

'Where?' I asked, feeling stupid for not being able to see them.

'Near that clearing, there . . .'

Now I saw them. These large animals were reduced to tiny dots in the majestic landscape.

Hghou! Hghou! came a new sound a distance away.

I looked at André, questioningly. 'Leopard!' he said excitedly. We soon found it with the binoculars, lazing on the sundrenched boulders on a nearby hill. Its elegant head was raised slightly off the rock, surveying the surroundings. Its spotted yellow coat shone golden in the sun. The tip of its long tail whisked around gently.

As we quenched our thirst with some of Mama's homemade fruit juice, Lwazi suddenly said the magic word. 'Elephants!'

CHAPTER 19

I counted five grey dots in the distance. They were moving through the trees at a lazy pace.

'Come!' shouted Themba. Soon we were back in the Land Rover, heading for the family of elephants.

I could see that even André and Simoshile shared in the excitement, even though they must have seen elephants a hundred times. The wind rushed by the Land Rover. Grabbing her hat, Moira giggled with tension and excitement.

And then . . . there they were . . . The giants of the bush. I held my breath. They were magnificent. Dusty grey. Enormous. Intelligent and immensely strong, I was sure. They seemed to be going about their business undisturbed. But every now and again you would see one of them shooting a quick glance in our direction. Shining black eyes. Yellow white tusks and a curious, curling trunk.

They moved around without a sound. 'Their massive feet have got very thick soles,' explained Themba, whispering now. 'It prevents them from slipping and it drowns out any noise should they step on a twig.'

'Why do they keep on flapping their ears?' asked Tom.

'Their ears have complex blood vessels. And if they fan them, it cools them down by as much as 5 °C.'

'They are so big . . .' said Moira.

'The bulls can weigh up to 6½ tons,' said Themba. 'But you probably would too if you ate 5% of your bodyweight in food every day!'

'Oh, I'm not sure if she doesn't already,' chuckled Frank. Moira gave him a deathly stare that would make even an elephant run for the hills.

The elephants seemed really peaceful. I was so taken in by them that I didn't even notice the tip of one of my fingers touching Simoshile's hand. But she did, and when I caught her looking at me weirdly, I pulled back my hand quickly, muttering, 'Sorry!'

We went back home for lunch and later rejoined the group for an afternoon drive through the Namhlanje camp. It was quite a tiring day, but we had seen so many animals: sable antelopes, jackal, zebras, baboons. And another one of the Big Five: buffalo.

Then, late that afternoon, as the sun was slipping down to the horizon, we heard the sound: Oemfff . . . Oemfff . . . Oemfff . . .

A sudden chill ran down my spine. It didn't seem to be very far off. I looked at André and Simoshile. Their faces tensed up.

'It's okay,' said André.

Themba's head turned towards his rifle, then back to the bush around us. Scanning it intently. He said a few words to Lwazi in isiZulu. I didn't understand it.

'What was that?' asked Moira, her face screwed up.

'Lions,' answered Themba, almost respectfully.

'Oh, my!' There was a slight alarm in Moira's voice.

'They're quite close. But don't worry.'

The Land Rover moved on slowly. I knew what Themba was thinking: It could be the lion they were looking for. What if it was him? Would he go chasing after it with the rest of us still seated at the back of the vehicle?

He seemed tense. Eventually Lwazi whispered, 'I see them.' His hand stretched out slowly. All heads turned in the direction he was pointing. My grip around the armrest tightened. Fear filled my mind.

There they were. A pride of about four lions. Two full-grown ones and two cubs. Their coats shone in the last glimmering light of day.

Again Themba and Lwazi exchanged words in isiZulu.

'It's not the one they're looking for,' whispered Simoshile to André and me.

The tense mood suddenly lifted as Themba's calm voice soothed our fears. 'The king of the animals,' he said with wonder.

The Americans insisted that the three of us join them for dinner that evening. Simoshile and André said they had to get back home. I looked at Themba, waiting for his approval. He nodded. 'Buyisiwe will join us,' he said. And a slight smile appeared on his lips. My heart skipped a beat.

There was a lovely campfire burning in the enclosure beside the main building. Themba called this place the lapa. It was beautifully decorated with candles, wooden African masks, carved statuettes, spears and animal hide shields. Mama Unahti moved about giving orders to her kitchen staff and seeing that everything ran according to plan. Her plan, of course!

The wonderful smell of food drifted in the air.

We were all gathered around the crackling fire. I sat next to Themba and marvelled at his charming ways with the guests.

They hung on his every word, as he explained the tough training game-rangers go through. 'We have to walk every road in the reserve, to get to know them better. It helps you memorise the features, like special trees, anthills, rocks, road junctions. These become your landmarks. You normally wouldn't even notice them when you drive around for the first time.'

He also set about explaining the exams they took: shooting practice, practical work like tracking animals and performing first aid.

'And you, son,' asked Moira, 'are you going to follow in your father's footsteps and become a Ranger too?'

'I . . . I don't know,' I stammered.

'All of this is new to Buyisiwe,' said Themba. 'He's been living in London all his life.'

'I thought your accent was a bit strange for an African,' said Moira.

I smiled, not knowing what to say.

'But he's getting used to living in Africa,' added Themba. 'He has already made some friends who seem to enjoy his company as well.'

There was a kindness in Themba's voice that I hadn't known before. Was he finally warming to me? Had I been wrong about him all this time?

A sudden drumbeat pierced the night. More beats followed, thumping in my chest. I looked around. Out of the dark appeared two drummers and six Zulu dancers. White, woolly fleece was tied to their lower legs and upper arms. Their loose hanging loincloths were made from brown animal hide. The tensed up muscles in their bare chests glimmered in the light of the fire. In their hands they carried spears and animal hide shields.

The tempo of the drumbeats increased, growing louder all the time. Pounding out a mesmerizing rhythm.

The dancers formed a half circle. Their bodies now moved as one. Twisting to the beat of the drum. Bare feet stomping, sending up clouds of dust. They whistled sharply. The beat changed, becoming dark, threatening, speaking to me in a language that only my heart seemed to understand.

I suddenly felt sad. But in a good way.

One of the dancers broke free from the group. He took centre stage. His eyes wide, body glistening with sweat. He danced, bending forward, and then curling over backwards again, muscles rippling. In a flash he raised his feet high up in the air, then he forced them down hard on the ground. The other dancers cheered him on, their spears banging against their shields. The dancer seemed to be in a trance, stomping his feet harder and harder until eventually he fell to the floor, exhausted. He scampered back to the others and another dancer broke free from the group, repeating the ritual.

All too soon it was finished. We all clapped hands. Frank cheered as the drummers and dancers disappeared back into the night.

'Were those real spears?' asked Moira with wide eyes.

Themba suppressed a smile. 'Yes, they were. The short spears that you saw were introduced by Shaka, the great Zulu king. The spears were called Iklwa because of the sound they made when you stabbed your enemy.'

'Oh, my!' said Moira softly. 'You say the king's name was Sa-ka?'

'Shaka,' corrected Themba. 'He was the founding father of the Zulu kingdom. He had a very unhappy childhood. He and his mother had both been driven from their home. Later he killed all of his paternal half brothers, except for three. Shaka ruled tyranically. When his mother, Nandi, died, Shaka lost his mind. He had hundreds of Zulus killed. And he ordered that no crops were to be planted or milk used for a whole year. He was eventually killed by two of his brothers, one of whom, Dingane, succeeded him.'

'Terrible!' said Moira with a sigh. 'I don't like stories of people getting killed. I'd rather you tell us an animal story!'

'All right, then. How about a story about the hippo?' asked Themba, his face shining like the sun, in the firelight. Moira nodded anxiously, like a little girl waiting for a bedtime story.

'Hippos had lived on land for centuries. But when, one day, they decided to settle in the water, the fish were the first to object: "You only want to eat us," they complained. "That's just silly," said the hippos. "We only eat grass. We need to cool down every once in a while. The African sun's rays are extremely hot. The water seems just the place to be." But the fish insisted that it was all a cleverly thought out plan to have them for breakfast, lunch and dinner. "All right then, we'll make you a deal," said the hippos. "If you allow us to make the water our home, we promise to always relieve ourselves on land. We'll spray our dung about and you will soon be comforted in seeing that there's not a single fish bone in it." And to this day, if you see a splattering of dung on a shrub or grass, you will know that it was left there by a hippo.'

'Lovely!' cried Moira, clapping her hands. We all laughed heartily. 'One more!' she cried.

'I think dinner is ready,' said Themba. 'Why don't we all enjoy Mama Unahti's lovely food, and afterwards I'll tell you how the giraffe got its long neck.'

We had barely finished dinner when Themba pulled me to the side. 'I think it's time for you to go to bed now, Buyi. Say goodnight and ask to be excused.'

'But I'm not tired yet.'

'Buyi, listen. I'm not asking you to do it, I'm telling you.' The strict tone was back in Themba's voice. It was all just a show then, all that careless banter in front of the guests. It made my heart sink. I did as he instructed.

Mama Unahti must have overheard Themba talking to me. She took me aside, and lovingly hugged me. 'Ngiyazi . . . I know,' she said, softly, warmly. 'I know . . .'

The road back to the chalet in the dark was long and lonely.

CHAPTER 20

As I passed Simoshile's chalet, I heard voices. They drew me nearer. She was sitting there with her dad, Lwazi. He had his arm around her shoulder. They were staring at the fire, their voices drifting in the wind. Mingling with the sound of the crickets and night birds.

I stood there in the dark, watching them. In that instant I realised what the love between a father and a child should be like. It pained me, for not having it with Themba. Was I being too hasty? Would it turn out all right eventually if I gave it some time?

I listened to the story Lwazi told Simoshile. It was a Zulu folktale about life and death. 'It was our great-great ancestor, uNkulunkulu, who created the Zulu people and the world around them. After making Man, he sent the chameleon off to pass on a joyful message to them: "You will bear a great number of children. And live forever." But then uNkulunkulu changed his mind, so he sent the gecko lizard off with another message: "All the people, all the animals, all living things will die!"

'The chameleon wandered off, lazily. He came upon some ubuKwébezane berries. They looked so good that he started feasting on them immediately. Time passed and still the chameleon ate berry after berry. There's still plenty of time left to deliver the message to Man, he thought. It was only much later that he decided to move on. When he eventually reached his destination, he found that the lizard had already delivered his message. And from that day on, all living things, including Man were doomed to die.'

The story stayed with me as I fell asleep that night, dreaming of chameleons and lizards.

I woke the following day with the sound of a plover screeching. The cicadas had also started their drawn-out jeer.

I felt a faint sadness inside me. Was I homesick? I missed Mum a lot. But I enjoyed South Africa. The animals, the people, the new experiences I would never have had back in London. I preferred the wide African skies to the dull, cloudy skies of London. I didn't miss the bustling streets of London, the grey buildings, the noise, the rain.

It was as if my soul had quietened down here. I could breathe freely. But there was still something missing . . .

I heard the front door open. Footsteps, which I recognised by now as Themba's.

'Buyi? Are you still sleeping?' he asked, leaning past the doorway into my room. His uniform was spotless.

'No, just lying here, thinking. What are you doing back?'

'I came to fetch my rifle. Lwazi, Johan and I are going out into the bush to try and find that lion. We had a bit of a scare yesterday. We don't want that to happen again.' He entered my room, glancing around. 'There are no guests in the camp today. The Americans have gone to the cheetah sanctuary down the road. They will be back late afternoon.'

'Can I come with you?' I sat upright in my bed.

'No!' His answer was abrupt.

I sighed and leaned back against the pillow. Another day of boredom.

'Why is this room such a pigsty?' Themba stared at me, his face strict, disapproving.

'Sorry?'

'All these things lying around. CDs, shoes, clothes . . . Didn't I tell you to do your washing? And clean up after yourself?'

'You told me to do my own washing. Not to clean up.'

'Do I have to spell everything out to you, Buyisiwe?' His voice was in attack mode. Fierce.

'Yes, why don't you? Then at least I would know what you want. Bloody hell!'

'You are not going to swear at me!'

'Oh, I'm sorry then, another thing you didn't spell out for me!'

Themba's whole body tensed up. His jaws were clenched. His hands rolled into tight fists. 'You will respect elder people. Get out of bed and get a move on. I'll be back this afternoon.' Silence fell between us, then he said, 'And another thing – make sure Umfana is cared for. See to it that he gets clean water and food. Clear enough for you?'

He left in a rage.

I felt the anger burning inside me. Bastard!

I got out of bed, banged the closet door shut, kicked the stuff lying about into one heap. I drew my finger over the desktop. The dirt stuck to my finger. The desk hadn't been cleaned since I got there. Neither had the tiles been mopped.

I was in no mood for this. I went to the kitchen to get myself a cup of coffee. While the water was busy boiling, I stepped outside to see to Umfana.

At least I knew somebody around there appreciated me.

The sun was already blazing down. The sand hot below my bare feet. I wiped away a weeping wattle branch from my face, the soft leaves tickling my skin. And then I saw something that made my heart stop.

The dog chain lay in a heap on the floor, partly covered by the yellow sand. Umfana was gone.

CHAPTER 21

It can't be, I told myself over and over again. I ran around the chalet, looking for Umfana. He wasn't there. The ground was covered in tracks. Old tracks, crumbling in. Disappearing.

'Umfana!' My cry rang out over the bush. 'Umfana!' I listened for his bark, a yelp. Anything.

Except for the normal sounds of the bush, there was nothing.

I couldn't believe it. How could he have broken free from his chain? The answer hit me: I hadn't tied him up! Two days ago, during that storm I'd let him into the house. Then Themba had arrived. I'd had to let him slip out the back door or I would have been in trouble.

Tie him up before he goes off killing animals.

That's what Themba told me that first time. I didn't listen. I just sent him off into the night. And now he was gone. It was entirely my fault. I needed to find him. Quick! But I would need help.

'You can't!' cried Simoshile. 'It is too dangerous.'

'I don't have a choice,' I said. 'I have to find him and I need you and André to help me!'

'There's a man-eating lion loose, Buyi. I'm not going to take that chance. I'm not going into any of the camps.'

'I'm your friend, aren't I?' I pleaded.

'Buyi is right,' said André. 'We have to help him.'

'He probably didn't wander too far,' I pleaded.

Simoshile crossed her arms and leaned back in the chair. 'I don't know. I'm scared.'

I looked at André. He frowned.

'We're scared too,' I said.

'Then don't go, Buyi. It is just a stupid dog. He'll come back.'

'It's been two days already. He might be lost.' Then softer, 'I don't want to lose him, Simoshile. Please, please . . .'

She thought it over a bit more, and then hesitantly gave in: 'Okay, I'll come with you.'

I felt terrible asking my friends to put their lives on the line for me. But I had no choice. I couldn't venture out into the bush alone. They were my age but they had way more experience than me.

André suggested that we start with the Namhlanje camp. It was the one bordering our chalet. If Umfana had wandered off into a camp, it would probably be that one.

'Umfana!' I called when we reached Namhlanje. My eyes scanned the land, peering at the tangled underbrush for signs of life. It was already scorching hot. I just hoped we had enough water to last us the day.

'Umfa – a – na – a!'

An hour went by. We found nothing. Once I saw the brown pelt of an animal move under a bush. I was just getting excited when it turned out to be a rabbit. It bounded off in a flash.

I didn't pay any heed to the many animals that we came across. The various antelope, giraffe, warthog . . . My mind was set on finding my dog.

But still . . . in the back of my mind there came the warning. The scarred lion is still out there. Be careful!

'Why didn't you ask your dad to help you find Umfana?' asked Simoshile.

'He doesn't know yet,' I stammered. 'He'll be furious.'

'Why do you say that? He seems like a kind man.'

'I . . . I just know.' I shrugged and shifted my attention back to the search. 'Umfana!' Desperation set in.

'I would have asked my dad if it was my dog that had got lost,' said Simoshile.

'Me too,' added André.

'The thing is . . .' I hesitated before continuing. 'Things between Themba and me . . . it's not too great.' I somehow felt relieved to get it out into the open. 'I know he is my dad and all, but we don't get along that well.'

'Have you talked to him about it?' asked Simoshile.

'No. We don't talk much either. I've been here for almost two weeks now, but he still seems like a stranger.' Silence. 'He still doesn't feel like my dad.'

'Have you told your mum?'

'No. I don't want her to worry.' I sighed. It was all too complicated.

'I would hate for you to leave,' said André, 'but if you and Themba don't get along . . . Perhaps it would be something worth considering.'

'That would be like copping out. I don't want to do that.' I looked at André, frowning.

'You remember that poster on my wall. The one with Amir Khan?'

'Yes?'

'You once asked me why I had it up.'

'And you said it was because you like boxing.'

I nodded. 'I've thought about it since. I think I look up to him because he is such an incredible fighter. He's got extraordinary vision and he doesn't let anything stand in the way of it. I want to be like him. I don't want to be a loser.'

Simoshile smiled quietly. She reached out her hand to me. I took it and it felt warm and comforting.

'Oh, please!' cried André, rolling his eyes. 'Are we looking for love here? Or are we looking for a dog?'

The moment was gone. We were back to the present. André was right; we had to find Umfana. It was already late morning and we hadn't made any progress.

Plodding along, our calls rang out without any success.

A terrible scream from Simoshile made my blood turn cold.

Umfana! I thought. She found him!

No. I followed her frightened eyes. 'Ibululu!' she said.

There was a snake right in front of my feet. Brown speckled. Short and stocky. Watching me.

'Puff adder, be careful,' whispered André. 'They're very dangerous!'

I didn't move, just kept my gaze fixed on the black eyes, the forked tongue darting in and out of its mouth. The seconds ticked by. It felt like hours. Then the puff adder lost interest and lazily slithered off.

'That was close,' sighed André. 'I hate them. They cause most of the snake bites in South Africa. And if they bite you, your body swells up to more than double its size.'

'You look like you've been dumped in boiling water, that's what my dad says,' added Simoshile. 'And the place where it bit you bursts open. Scary! Really scary!'

I shivered. 'And can you die?'

'Hell, yeah!' cried André.

'It could also have been something else,' said Simoshile softly.

'It was a puff adder,' said André irritated. 'It's not the first time I've seen one, Simoshile. And you said it yourself.'

'No, that's not what I mean.' We frowned, gazing at her. 'In the Zulu culture we believe that our ancestors sometimes appear to us in the form of snakes.'

'Ancestors?' I asked.

'Their spirits, really. Ancestors play a huge role in our culture. If they appear to you as a dangerous snake they'll behave peacefully. Sometimes you can recognise them by the marks carried on the snake's body.'

'Okay, now you really are scaring me,' I said. 'What would they want from us?'

'Not from us, Buyi – from you. The puff adder had its eyes fixed on you.'

A shiver ran down my spine. 'What would they possibly want from me?' I stammered.

Simoshile was now deadly serious. 'Buyi, the ancestors may have come to warn you of danger lying ahead.'

CHAPTER 22

I stared at Simoshile. Danger? Should we get out of the camp? But what about Umfana? We had to find him. Pangs of guilt still haunted me for not taking better care of him.

'I could be wrong,' she added. 'But . . . what if I'm not?'

'I don't believe in any of that nonsense,' said André. 'It was just a snake that stared at Buyi's ugly mug for a while and then slithered off. Nothing more. Let's get a move on and find Umfana. I think we must try the erosion area. There's lots of hiding places for a dog there.'

We changed direction and made our way through a rough piece of land. Simoshile's words still played on my mind. I felt unsettled and tried to pass the incident off as unimportant. Since when did I start to believe in ghosts, or ancestors or whatever?

Around us the sun glistened on the leaves. The treebark was dotted with grey-green lichen. We shouted Umfana's name. But still we had no success.

Then we reached the erosion area. It was like a surreal moonscape. A ravine curling through the land. Its sand-coloured walls covered in gothic-like structures. Towers, crevices, cracks, small caves. We climbed down into the ravine. The ground was like clammy sea sand. André stopped to examine the tracks left behind by animals. His finger drew an arrow shape around one of the tracks, and a Christmas tree shape around the other. He shook his head.

'Impala and jackal, I think.'

'I've never liked this place,' said Simoshile, crossing her arms. 'It's scary.'

'We'll be okay,' comforted André. I nodded as if I knew he was right.

The sand crunched below our feet as we marched on.

'Umfana!' My voice returned to me, echoing back from the ravine wall.

We searched the nooks and crannies of the rough walls. But there were way too many of them. If Umfana had fallen down one of the cracks we might never find him. It all seemed like a useless exercise. I hated to, but eventually I had to concede: 'I think we should turn back.'

'Shouldn't we go on a bit longer? At least till lunch?' asked André.

'We'll never find him. The game resort is just too big. It's like searching for a needle in a haystack.'

André seemed disappointed. I was too, but what else could we do?

It was then that we heard the roar of an engine. My heart stopped. 'Hide!' I cried.

I was just about to head for one of the small caves when André said: 'What? Are you stupid? Look around you . . .'

He was right. Our footsteps lay scattered all over the place. It would be child's play finding us in there.

Moments later the Land Rover appeared at the top of the ravine. Then Themba, Lwazi, and Johan came into view. They all had guns with them.

We stared up at them. There was nothing we could do. There were no excuses we could give. We were in trouble.

'It's all my fault,' I said when we reached the top of the ravine. We stood before the three uniformed men. I stared down at my shoes. 'I asked for their help.'

'Help with what?' asked Themba angrily.

'Umfana. He ran away.'

'What! But I told you . . .'

'I know.'

'Get in the Land Rover!' shouted Themba. 'We'll talk when we get home.'

I felt dreadful. Empty. Scared. I could sense my two friends felt the same. We didn't speak a word. The fearful looks we exchanged said it all.

The tension was unbearable. We dropped the others off. Themba and I drove home alone. On our way there Themba suddenly stopped the Land Rover. He sat staring at the dust road ahead. His hands clenched around the steering wheel. I could see a jaw muscle tensing up. I looked away.

'Why don't you just listen?' he exploded suddenly. 'Is it that hard to understand,

Buyisiwe? There's a lion out there. It has already attacked a man. It has killed another.'

'But . . .'

'No, listen! You thought you could take a chance and go off into the bush on foot. What if you came across the lion? Did you think you could run away from it? Lions cover more ground in two bounds than humans do in ten. You would have no chance against it.'

'But Umfana . . .' I stammered.

'Forget about the miserable dog! I'm talking about you now! This isn't London, Buyisiwe. This is Africa. Things are different here. Life and death . . . they go hand in hand here.

'That lion is old. He probably got into a terrible fight and was exiled from his pride. That's where the scar came from. But he won't give up that easily. Survival – that's all that matters to him. He is ruled by his age-old instincts. They urge him to feed.

Once a lion has attacked and eaten one man, he'll do it again. We are easy prey for him now. It's as simple as that.'

I couldn't look Themba in the eye. His voice was relentless.

'Have you ever seen a lion attack and kill its prey? If it leaps out at you it will knock you right back . . . it could break your neck. Or it might seize you by the throat, its incisors tearing into your flesh, your arteries. Closing down the blood flow to your brain. You already start losing consciousness as it drags you down. Helpless against its might. You wouldn't even have time to cry for help. It would be over in a flash. It will tear out your entrails first, and eat them. Then it'll have a go at your legs. Finally it will move its way up to your head, crushing your skull like it was a can of Coke!'

I shrunk back in the seat.

'No, don't look away now, my boy. You think you are so clever. This is what will happen to you.'

'I'm sorry,' I whispered.

'Sorry just won't cut it, Buyi.' He inhaled deeply. The whites of his eyes were showing. As his breathing steadied, his voice quieted down. 'Why did you do it? Why did you go after the dog?'

The thoughts rushed around in my mind. I was afraid. Should I tell him? The answer fell out: 'Because I loved him. Because . . . he was there for me when you weren't.'

I thought Themba would go off again. I thought he would grab me by the throat and strangle the life right out of me. Go feed me to the scarfaced lion. But he didn't.

It was as if a veil suddenly dropped between us. When he yelled at me only moments ago, he was so real. He was a human being. At last I had seen a man filled with emotion. And even though it was hurtful hearing him say those things, I felt closer to him than ever.

But now I could sense him pulling back emotionally again. Something was wrong. I just knew it. But what it was, I couldn't tell.

'Let's go find your dog,' he finally said. His words nearly knocked the wind right out of me.

There were no further words between us as we drove in the direction of the camp.

He was there for me when you weren't.

I shouldn't have said that. How could I? I was stupid! Now he's going to hate me even more. I shot a quick sideways glance at him. It was useless. I couldn't read what was going on in his mind.

A bead of sweat ran down his temple. His black face shining in the afternoon sun. The Zulu warrior.

I didn't know the culture. What if we weren't really on our way to look for the dog? What if it is expected to discipline children who speak ill of their fathers? Or worse – what if it is expected to kill them?

I wouldn't know.

My hands were sweating. I looked at Themba's rifle. No, I am mistaken. He wouldn't do something like that. I could barely think now. All around us lay the beautiful South African landscape. But this all faded into the background. Fear had taken its place.

We drove down one dirt road after another. I pretended to look for Umfana. I even shouted his name a few times. My voice sounded weak.

'Umfana! Umfana!'

We stopped numerous times. Themba got out of the Land Rover and inspected the ground. Looking around for tracks. When he climbed back in, he would switch the Land Rover on again and drive further.

I didn't want to ask him what he saw. If anything at all. Then, after what seemed like our twentieth stop, he appeared to have found something. He got back into the Land Rover and turned off the road. We headed through the grassland, past clumps of trees where fallen dry branches cracked under the tyres. We stopped another three times.

What I didn't know was that death was only a heartbeat away. That every stop brought us closer to it.

Life and death . . . they go hand in hand here.

Themba saw him first. He stopped suddenly. Did he gasp for air, or was it only the wind? And was it that same wind that carried the faint yelping sounds towards me?

'Umfana?'

I got out of the Land Rover. My legs felt weak. Where was he? My eyes followed Themba as he headed up a narrow footpath to a thicket.

And then I saw him. Horror rushed through my body. Could this be? I ran to Umfana, but stopped short, kneeling down a short distance away from the dog. I felt the nausea pushing up into my throat.

Still the yelps sounded. Begging me to come closer. To help.

I crawled to him on my hands and knees. Tears were now streaming down my face.

I touched his head. Gently. A rush of pain shot through me. I stared down at the blood covering my fingers.

'What happened, boy?'

But I knew. I knew. The open wound ran right around his neck. Flesh exposed, cut by the piece of wire tied to a tree. Like a noose.

He had been caught in one of the poacher's traps.

The poachers don't care if they hurt the animals. And if they catch something that they don't want, they just leave it there to die.

That's what Themba told the American visitors yesterday.

I felt anger burning inside me now. It consumed me. I wanted to scream. Cry. Swear.

But all I could do was hurt.

Gently I loosened the wire noose. I slipped it off Umfana's neck. He lay there unmoving in his own blood. His eyes were distant. His breathing shallow.

I ran back to the Land Rover and fetched a water bottle. I poured small amounts of it into the palm of my hand. Hoping that he would lap it up. That it would make him stronger.

But he didn't respond. I watched the water run through my fingers, disappearing into the dry sand.

'There's nothing we can do for him,' said Themba.

I dreaded those words. Deep inside me I knew Themba was right. I didn't want to believe it. But seeing Umfana's wounds made it all too true.

I lifted Umfana's head onto my lap. Stroked the soft coat, curled my fingers around his ears like I had done that first day I saw him.

'I'm so sorry,' I whispered. 'I should have taken better care of you. I let you down.' I couldn't stop the tears.

I heard Themba move away to the Land Rover. Moments later he returned. The sudden cock of a rifle behind me made me jump.

I looked up, right into the sun. Shielding my eyes, I saw Themba's silhouette behind me. The rifle held out towards me.

'He's your dog. You have to put him out of his misery.' The words fell like sharp rocks, burying me.

'Themba?'

'Shoot him!'

CHAPTER 23

'No!'

'There's nothing we can do for him.'

'I know, but . . .'

'Shoot him, Buyi! He's your dog. Finish it!' He pushed the rifle into my hands. A shock went through me. I had never touched a rifle before. It was heavy, warm from the sun.

'I can't.'

'Are you a man?' His voice was cold.

'Yes.' Softly.

'Do you want Umfana to suffer further?'

'No.'

'Then do it! Now!'

I couldn't believe it was happening. Themba was cruel. Heartless. How I hated him. I knew he didn't care for me. This proved it.

'Pull the rifle butt into your shoulder. Your cheek here . . .' He showed me. I felt his chest against my back. Smelled his sweat. Felt the power in his arms as he guided my arms, my hands.

And I trembled. Even on the inside. Every cell in my body cried: No! No! No!

Umfana's body aligned with the rifle sight. I saw the look in his eyes. Was it terror? Or relief, knowing what was about to happen?

Terrifying seconds ticked by.

'Breathe steady,' said Themba.

No! No! No!

'Squeeze the trigger, gently.'

'No!' I cried. The powerful sound of my voice rang out across the bush.

I held the rifle out to Themba, and turned my head away. I didn't want him to see me crying.

He took the rifle from me. I sank my head into my hands and walked away. Still shaking. Horrified. But relieved, until . . .

The gunshot rang out.

I was stunned by its intensity. Sudden. Sharp. Thundering back from the mountains.

My mouth fell open. I stopped breathing. I stopped thinking. Lost. Empty. Silent.

Themba turned to me. His jaws clenched. His face relentless. 'You're not a man,' he said.

'I hate you,' I said under my breath.

'Did you find him?' asked André as he and Simoshile came running. Themba and I had just arrived back at the chalet.

I nodded. My face felt swollen from all the crying.

'Where is he?' asked Simoshile.

I stared back at the rifle in the Land Rover.

Simoshile's lips parted slightly. She brought her hand up to her mouth. Eyes wide.

'Sorry,' said André softly.

Simoshile put her arm around me. I shrugged it off. 'Leave me alone!'

She was shocked. I was too. I never thought I would say something like that to somebody who cared for me.

'I . . . I want to be alone,' I tried again. I couldn't look at her. I was ashamed, but also filled with sadness. 'I just need some time, okay Simoshile?'

She nodded.

'We'll see you soon,' said André. He took Simoshile by the arm and they left. Simoshile looked back once. There were tears in her eyes.

I looked down at my bloodstained hands. These were the hands I had used to dig Umfana's grave. The hands I had used to gently place his body inside.

I clenched my fists. They fell open again in an instant. I was drained.

And never before had I felt so alone.

Themba washed up, then drove off, back to the main buildings. I was thankful that he wasn't there with me in the chalet. I knew he would come back sooner or later. Then I would have to face him. I dreaded that moment.

I ambled around the chalet, aimlessly. I hadn't had anything to eat since that morning. And I didn't feel like eating anything now.

I was not as tough as I thought I was. I was just a meek boy. I had nothing in common with this land, these people.

I remembered how I'd felt about London. That I didn't belong there. But now I knew that I didn't belong in South Africa either. When I landed here I didn't feel a connection with the land. And still there was no connection.

I didn't really come home.

I didn't really return, like my name suggested.

I was no one. And that was probably why Themba treated me the way he did.

The phone rang. I didn't want to answer, but it kept on ringing. Eventually I picked it up.

'Yes?'

'Buyi? Is that you?'

My heart lifted for only a moment. 'Mum! I'm so glad to hear your voice.'

'What's wrong?' I kept quiet. 'Buyi, tell me.'

'I've had a bad day.'

'What happened?'

Deep breath. 'He . . . he doesn't like me.' Finally I dared to say those words. 'And I don't care for him either.'

'But have you tried?'

'He wanted me to shoot Umfana today! Why should I try? I hate him.'

I could hear the worry in her voice. 'I'll talk to him.'

'It's no use.'

'Of course it is.'

Seconds ticked by without either of us saying anything. I listened to Mum's breathing. Just knowing she was there at the other end of the line comforted me.

'And how have you been doing?' I asked eventually.

The answer took a long time coming: 'Miserable. I miss you a lot, Buyi.'

'And I miss you.'

'I've tried to sound cheerful whenever I talk to you. And I know I've been telling you how everything is fine, but really, it isn't.'

'Mum?'

'I've been struggling to get through my days without you, Buyi.'

'Why didn't you tell me?'

'I didn't want to upset you. I knew you had a lot on your plate now.'

So, we both acted the same. Both of us so careful of the other's feelings. Not wanting to hurt the other.

Later, as I lay on my bed thinking it all over again, the decision slowly surfaced in my mind: I'm going back to London.

CHAPTER 24

Driven by anger, I jumped up from my bed. I had to do it. I had to get away from there. Themba wouldn't miss me. Hell, he might even be glad that I was gone.

His face flashed before me. He had the same look in his eyes as that afternoon when he handed me the rifle.

Shoot him, Buyi! He's your dog. Finish it!

How could a father ask that of his son? I had no answer, only determination now. I simply had to get away.

But how? Pacing up and down in my room I made a plan. First I had to get out of the resort. The main gate would be the obvious choice. Straight out and down that dust road I arrived on. But there was a guard at the gate. He would get suspicious and alert Themba. And before I could even get to the gate, others might see me as well. Visitors, Mama Unahti, one of the rangers, André, Simoshile . . .

No, I couldn't just walk out the main gate. I had to take a different route. In my mind I pictured the three wildlife camps bordering the main camp.

There was another way of getting out of there. I had to make my way through the Kusasa camp. It bordered the dust road to the resort on one side. If I could take a short cut through Kusasa, and meet up with the dust road further along, I would be okay. From there on I would make my way to the tarred road and try and catch a lift to Bela-Bela, and then onto the highway and straight to the airport.

The plane ticket. How would I get a plane ticket? The question lingered in my mind. I still had a bit of money left, some savings stashed away in a British bank. If I needed to, I could use that to help pay for the ticket back to London.

I had to hurry. The sun had already started slipping down to the horizon. I had to get to the dust road before dark.

I couldn't take along all of my stuff. A backpack would have to do. A few items of clothing. My passport. Some food. A torch and pliers – I would have to cut the wire fence when I reached the resort's border.

I suddenly wished I could say goodbye to André and Simoshile. They had become dear friends these past days. Mama Unahti too. And Lwazi. But I couldn't risk it. I sighed. Feeling the loss of true friendship already. I'd write them a letter when I got back home, I decided.

As I looked around my room one final time, I felt that emptiness inside me yet again. Then my eyes found the picture of Amir Khan. A flood of feelings rushed through me. But somehow shame was the one surfacing above all the others. I couldn't live up to the dream of triumphantly fighting my battles.

Back at school I could raise my fists and throw a mean punch. But the greatest battles are fought on the inside. And those were the ones I couldn't win.

I had let myself down but there was nothing I could do about it now.

Stepping out of the chalet, I glanced in the direction of Umfana's kennel. And then, under cover of the trees, I walked on, all the while making sure nobody saw me.

I am leaving it all behind now, I said to myself. You are going to be okay, Buyi. This is not the end. It is a new beginning.

But a voice from the back of my mind kept on taunting me: Run-away! Couldn't handle it, could you? You're not a man!

I tried to shake the voice. I had to concentrate.

Up ahead the Kusasa gate came into view.

CHAPTER 25

The leaves and grass tinted orange. The bark of the trees became black silhouettes against the setting sun. A sweet, mellow scent rose out of the earth like ancient burning incense. A light breeze cooled the air. The call of the birds became sharper as the bush was settling in for the night.

I kept my head up. I knew which direction I had to take. It is not that far, I said to myself.

Dry leaves and twigs crackled under my shoes. Intently listening to the regular pace kept me company. Soothed my thoughts.

I don't know why but Simoshile suddenly entered my mind. I thought back to the marula tree. The marriage tree. I remembered the moment we shared that morning as we held hands. Hers was soft in mine.

'Get a grip on yourself!' I reproached myself out loud. 'You're never going to see her again.'

The very thought made my body ache.

But it was true. I had to get a move on. It was getting dark; I had to keep my mind focussed.

I made sure I was still on track and then quickened my pace.

A sudden sound a few feet away made me jump. Just in time I saw the warthog scampering off, its tail erect. It was probably busy digging for tasty roots when I disturbed it.

I tried to settle my mind again, gain control of my breathing.

The way to the camp's border seemed further now. Doubt filled my mind. Was I on the right track? Perhaps I had been mistaken. Perhaps this wasn't the right direction at all. I stopped, stared back where I'd come from. Everything looked the same now.

It was getting darker still.

You can't afford to hesitate now, Buyi, I said to myself.

I went on in the direction I had followed earlier. Hoping that it was the right one.

My backpack bore down heavily on my shoulders. I gritted my teeth. You'll show Themba what you're capable of. You're not going to give up now. And you're certainly not going to hang around and let him mess with your mind.

Oemfff!

The sudden sound stopped me in my tracks.

Oemfff!

It was unmistakable. A lion!

My heart raced. No, not here, not now, I silently begged. This was supposed to be the safer camp of the three.

It is not him, it is not the one with the scar, I tried consoling myself, hoping that I was right.

Oemfff!

The sound vibrated in my chest, in every bone in my body. It was like a sound system turned up to its full volume. It left me breathless for a moment.

What was I to do? Turn back and hope he hadn't noticed me? Or move forward?

I had already covered a lot of ground now. It was way too far to turn back. The road ahead was still uncertain, the distance to the border fence unknown.

Just go on, find the fence! Get out of here!

I pulled out my torch and switched it on. Then I strode forward. It soon turned to a jog. The light bounced around on the ground.

Oemfff!

Where was the lion? To my left I think. But the first roar was more to the back. Was I running in a circle? The very thought was like a kick in the guts.

That's what you get for being a smart-ass.

Suddenly my foot caught on a rock. I stumbled and fell forward. The torch flew out of my hands. It died as it hit the ground.

Thorns tore into my palms. I could feel the blood running down my arms. It hurt, but I got up again.

Blood – would the lion be able to smell it?

There was a slight breeze coming from the right. I turned my head towards it. If the lion was still on my left, it probably meant that he could smell me.

Horrifying thought.

Lions are most dangerous at night, that is what André had said. Lwazi had also warned me: *lions become totally different animals at night. It is their hunting time . . .*

I prayed that I would be safe. But would I?

We had come across that snake earlier today – Simoshile said it could be an ancestor coming to warn me of danger. I didn't believe in that crap. But now it seemed all too true.

Oemfff! Oemfff!

I crossed my arms over my chest, trying to stop the incredible reverberation. Even my insides seemed to shiver with every powerful roar.

The sound now came from the right. Was he circling me? Trying to find the right moment to attack?

The strangest smell hit me right in the face. An odour so strong, I knew it could only be him.

My senses were on high alert, as I was sure his were too. I had now heard him, caught his pungent scent . . . But I was yet to see him. He stayed back, but haunting thoughts warned me: he was watching me from the dark. Stalking me.

I didn't want to run. It would be futile. He could catch up with me in seconds if he wanted to.

I stood there transfixed, a numbing fear in my heart.

I thought the tension couldn't mount any more, but then suddenly: two eyes, flashing briefly in the dark.

It scared me even further. He was not that far off. And he was staring right at me!

I panicked. Staggered back, fell and scrambled to my feet again. My backpack was heavy. I ripped it off and dropped it at my feet.

The hunter and the prey. I was now caught in the age-old game of survival. And the lion hadn't even made his first move yet.

I could hear my own heartbeat, the rush of blood in my ears, a strange sound escaping my lips.

I remembered Lwazi telling us that lions sometimes just want to scare people off. They would head straight for someone, just to stop short in a cloud of dust.

I hoped this would be the case here too, but somehow I doubted it. I was a mere animal to him. Not a person, to be afraid of. This was his territory. And I was nothing but dinner.

If I was going to die that night, I just hoped it would be a quick death. And painless. But how painless could it be, having your stomach ripped open, your head cracked?

The terror raging inside me momentarily blinded me from everything else but me and the lion.

And then a search light shone over the bush. It jerked me back to a bigger reality, where there was more to the world than a scarred lion and a teenage boy.

There came the roar of an engine. The vehicle approached. The light fell over me, but only for a moment. Then it moved away, across the field. And it stopped, pinned on the lion. Tawny, strong, bushy dishevelled mane. The scar above his left eye.

He was still watching me. Now I could see his piercing yellow eyes. The powerful jaws. Muscles rippled underneath his coat.

'Buyi, stay calm.' It was Themba's voice. Soft, commanding. 'It's going to be okay. Don't make a sudden move. Don't run.'

'It's him!' I stuttered.

'I know.' Themba was now approaching on foot. Carefully. I caught sight of him from the corner of my eye. He had a rifle with him. His other hand outstretched as if to calm me.

'You'll be fine,' said another voice. It was Lwazi's. He was standing behind the searchlight.

Easy for you to say, I thought. But then I realised I was wrong. Lwazi had already had an encounter with this lion. And he had lived to tell the tale. I could too.

'Calm, stay calm,' said Themba. 'Don't look him in the eye, Buyi. He would see it as a challenge. Keep your head down.'

I dropped my head, but my eyes kept on tearing back to the lion. I had to know if he was about to charge.

The lion took one careful step closer. My heart jumped.

'Stay calm . . .' said Themba.

Another step.

'Take a deep breath. You'll be okay.'

Closer.

The lion's dark mane moved across his shoulders and head. His eyes flashed. Fearless yellow eyes lined with black. His jaws opened for a second; exposing the sharp, white incisors.

'No!' I cried. The word slipped out before I could stop it. Fear had got the better of me.

I crumbled.

A yellow streak of lightning. Power, speed and death rolled into one.

Themba moved in-between me and the lion. A shield.

The lion leaped forward. Claws out. A roar escaped his throat, echoing through the night. Shaking the earth below me.

The lion struck Themba square on the chest. The rifle flew from his hands. A shot went off from the impact as the rifle hit the ground.

Themba crashed down on me. The lion was there too, pinning us both to the ground. His mighty body crushing us.

Again the roar. Muscles rippling.

I gasped for breath, choking on the billowing cloud of sand enfolding us.

We're going to die!

The claws ripped through the skin on Themba's face. The lion's jaws opened. The pink insides of its mouth, its tongue, razor-sharp teeth right before me. Saliva glistening.

And then the shot!

CHAPTER 26

The sound shattered the night. First the loud bang, and almost immediately after the thud! Then all went quiet. No birds, no crickets or scurrying animals. No voices, no breathing.

Just silence. And billowing dust.

I lay there on my back, watching the moon slide out from behind a cloud. The cloud seemed almost translucent, the moon somehow magical.

I was alive! Alive! Once this incredible thought had struck me, I slowly tried to move my limbs. As if to make sure that it wasn't just a dream.

There was a heavy weight on top of me. Themba and the lion. Seeing them both from up close was strange. It was as if I had snapped out of a nightmare, only to realise that it was all true. I'd been attacked by a lion and Themba had saved me.

Themba.

Was he okay? His eyes were closed. His body as still as the lion's.

No!

Hurried footsteps kicked up some more dust around us. 'Buyi! Themba! Are you hurt?' I was thankful hearing Lwazi's voice again.

'Okay . . . I'm okay,' I whispered, my mouth dry and throbbing with pain. I had bitten down on the inside of my cheek during the fall.

'Themba?' Lwazi stood astride us. His arms strained at the lion's heavy body, trying to drag it aside. He clenched his teeth against his own pain. His shoulder had not healed completely. Heaving the mighty lion off my dad, he called out to him again: 'Themba!'

I finally managed to free myself completely. Lwazi rolled Themba over on his back. Solemnly. Silently. He shot a quick glance at me, and then placed his ear to Themba's mouth. Listened . . .

'He's alive!' They were the sweetest words I've ever heard. 'We have to get him to a hospital.' Lwazi ran back to the Land Rover. I heard him calling for help on the radio. His voice the only sound in the clear night.

I kneeled beside Themba. 'Dad . . .' I whispered. It was the first time I'd called him that. The word felt strange on my tongue. 'It's going to be okay. Just hang in there!'

I looked down at his body. It was covered in blood. His clothes torn, exposing deep gashes. And then the cut on his forehead . . .

Just like the scarred lion's.

'Ngonyama . . .' The first word Themba said, as he slowly opened his eyes in the hospital. 'Ngonyama . . .'

I frowned as I looked down at him. I didn't know what he meant.

The doctor had given him something for the pain. He was calm now. The operation to fix his internal wounds had been a success. The gash on his forehead was closed and bandaged. 'It will take time for it to heal. There'll be a scar. But we can fix it later with plastic surgery,' said the doctor.

I smiled at Themba. 'How are you doing?'

'Fine,' he whispered bravely. The word fragile, like porcelain. 'And you?'

'I'm okay. Just a few cuts and bruises. Mama Unahti has been taking care of me.'

He nodded slowly, closed his eyes and drifted off to sleep again, smiling.

Waking up the following day, he had more of his wits about him. His eyes seemed more alive, he could even move his arms and legs.

'You still here?'

'Yes, Dad. I stayed through the night.' We stared at each other for a while. 'Go-ya-ma . . .' I said. 'That's what you said yesterday. When you came around.'

He frowned at first, but then realised what I'd tried to say. 'Ngonyama.'

'Yeah, that, what does it mean?'

'It's my surname.' Of course! I had heard André calling him Mister Ngonyama once. 'It is isiZulu for lion.'

'Oh?'

He took a deep breath. His lip quivered. 'My ancestral tribe had been assigned the task . . . the sacred duty of protecting lions. And taking care of the other animals living with them. Ensuring that they didn't come to any harm.' His voice was now filled with strained emotion. 'And I've failed . . . I've failed the lions.'

I took his hand. It was warm in mine.

'No, you didn't,' I said softly. His eyes looked at me, questioningly. 'You protected me.'

'Buyi?' He still didn't understand.

'Okay, I know my surname is Johnson, that's how Mum registered it. But I'm your son. Ngonyama – I'm one too. A lion. And you saved me.'

His hand tightened around mine. I could see him biting back the tears.

'I'm sorry I ran away.' My voice was soft, trembling. 'I . . . I wanted to go back home to Mum. After everything that happened . . . I just didn't want to stay in South Africa anymore.'

'I was too rough on you.'

'It's hard for me to say but I . . . I felt like I didn't belong, that you didn't want me here.'

Again he bit back the tears, but it was no use. They were now streaming down his face. He turned his head away. His shoulders were shaking.

'It's okay,' I whispered.

Composing himself, he looked at me again. 'You know, it's funny, the Swahili people say that when a lion roars, it's actually saying: Whose land is this? Mine, mine, mine! And it should be yours too.'

A jolt went through me.

'I've watched you these past couple of days,' continued Themba. 'You've changed since you came here. Africa has been good for you. You belong here.'

'I don't know.'

'It's true – Africa can be a tough place. It's been that way since Man could remember. A lot of blood has been spilt here. These people, all of them, black and white have known hardship. But they are real people. Warm. Loving.'

You weren't, I wanted to say, but didn't. I only stared down at his hand. He must have sensed what I felt. 'I was so scared,' he said, his voice trailing off to a thoughtful silence.

I frowned. 'Scared?'

'That I would lose you.' Again the silence. 'Having you here has been hard on me too. I've never had to care for anybody but myself.'

'And the wild animals in the resort,' I added.

'Caring for animals is different from caring for people. Then you came along. And boy, was that a shock!' He smiled. I did too. 'That first day I saw you . . . I got scared thinking that you were now my responsibility. And I was clueless. How do you care for a child? Your own child!'

'I thought you didn't like me.'

'That's not true. Please believe me. I liked you since I set eyes on you. But it was so strange having you around when I came home. You must remember that I have always lived alone. During the day I entertained lots of people, telling them about the bush, the animals. And when I got home, there was always this silence. Loneliness.

'It all changed when you came. And I felt like a failure, not being able to talk to you like a father would talk to his son.'

'I didn't know what to say to you either.'

'I am sorry for not making you feel more welcome, Buyi.'

I nodded.

We stared at each other for a while. That terrifying moment with the lion had changed things between us. Staring death in the eye does that to people. You take stock of your life and begin to see what is important to you.

'Has your mother ever told you how we met?' Themba asked.

'No.'

I could almost see the memories come flooding back to him. 'I was a young man. In my early twenties. I had barely finished my training as a game-ranger. I got a job at a game resort. Not Isigubhu where I am now, one further to the north. It was the opportunity of a lifetime.

'And then one day a group of tourists arrived. From England. Your mum was one of them. She was so beautiful. We hit it off right away.'

'Soul mates?' I asked.

'Yes, some people call it that.' Themba sighed. 'But it was not to be. The resort forbade any contact, other than professional, with guests. But how do you forbid love? As the devil would have it, we got caught. I was given a disciplinary hearing. I lost my job. Your mum had to go back to London . . .' Themba's face dropped as if he could still feel the pain.

'Why didn't you go with her?'

'I had no money. And times were different then.'

'But did you at least keep in contact?'

'Yes. And then one day she phoned me with the news. She was two months pregnant. I was overjoyed. My parents, however, were not.'

'You still have parents?' I asked.

'Not anymore. They died a few years back.'

'Oh.'

'They forbade me to see your mum. They wanted me to take an African woman as a wife. And so it was that we drifted apart. We each got on with our lives. I found a new job. In the back of my mind I began to realise that I might never get to see my child. Your mum phoned me again the day after you were born. I asked her to call you Buyisiwe.'

'Returned.'

Themba nodded. 'And for years we lost contact, until . . .'

'. . . recently when Mum ran into money trouble.'

Themba nodded.

'Do you still love her?'

'I don't know. It's been so long. But I have never loved anyone like I did your mother once.'

Taking stock of our lives: that is what the lion attack did.

CHAPTER 27

A knock at the hospital room door made me look up.

'What is this? Are you still in bed, Themba?' cried Lwazi cheerfully. 'But it was just a scratch!'

The others crowded behind him: André and Simoshile, followed by Mama Unahti, carrying flowers and a tin of cookies.

'Not everybody is as stubborn as you are, Lwazi,' said Mama Unahti, clicking her tongue. 'Can you believe it, Themba? He still hasn't taken all his medicine.'

'I am as strong as an ox,' said Lwazi. 'I don't need medicine!'

'Eish! I wish there was a pill for stubbornness!'

Mama Unahti and Lwazi laughed heartily and put their arms around each other. I had always thought there was something going on between the two of them. But now I was sure.

'Don't mind them, Mister Ngonyama,' said Simoshile, rolling her eyes with shame. 'They're like two school children these days. How are you?'

'I'm fine thank you, Simoshile.'

'Tell us about the lion!' said André. His face was alight with expectation.

'Didn't Buyi tell you?' asked my dad.

'Yeah, he did, but I want to hear your side of the story now. Just in case the Englishman left something out.'

'Englishman? I don't know if you can call him that anymore, André. After the lion attack, I think he is more African, than English. What do you say, Buyi?'

I shrugged and smiled.

Then Themba became more serious. 'But there is something you guys need to know. Buyi told me that he would like to go back to London.'

'No! You can't!' cried Simoshile.

Everybody stared at her in amazement. She became shy suddenly.

'Oh, it's the love thing again,' grinned André, elbowing me.

'Love thing, André?' frowned Themba.

'Didn't you know, Mister Ngonyama?'

'Don't listen to him, Dad. He's just teasing,' I said.

'No, I'm not!' cried André. 'I saw them holding hands!'

'Well, well,' said Mama Unahti clasping her hands. 'Lwazi, your little girl is in love!'

Lwazi looked a bit confused. But his face lit up as he shifted his gaze to Simoshile. She smiled, took my hand and gave me a quick peck on the cheek.

'Oh no!' cried André sticking out his tongue and screwing up his face.

A warm jolt of lightning went right through me. It was strange being kissed by a girl. Even a quick kiss like the one she gave me. I could still feel her soft lips pressing against my cheek. 'Thanks,' I said and smiled sheepishly.

Thanks. Was that the best I could do? But what else do you say?

The others just laughed at me.

'Looks like you have no choice but to stay a while longer, Buyi,' said Themba. 'You wouldn't want to break a young girl's heart now, would you?'

I gently squeezed Simoshile's hand, looked into her kind eyes and said, 'You're right, Dad. I couldn't do that.' Simoshile smiled. 'But . . .' Her smile faded again. My troubled gaze shifted back to Themba.

'Your mother . . .' he said. I nodded. 'Why don't you give her a call when you get back to the resort.'

'Call her?'

'Yes. Tell her to come over for a visit. I'll somehow scrape together some money to pay for the plane ticket. It would be great to see her again. And if she still likes South Africa as much as she did back then . . . who knows, we'll take it from there.'

Driving back to the game resort later that afternoon, I thought about all that had happened to me. The hard times and the good.

I gazed out at the sundrenched sky, the rustling trees, the gracious land and I thought: Africa is more than a landscape – it is a sense-scape. It beckons you to listen, see, smell, touch, taste and experience.

I looked at Simoshile sitting alongside me and I knew I would be all right. I belonged here in South Africa. And I could roar it loud, just like the lion: Whose land is this? Mine, mine, mine!